PAINT IT BLACK

SARAH JANE HUNTINGTON

For Sorren and Alfie the dog, he was a very good boy.

VELOX BOOKS
Published by arrangement with the author.

Paint It Black copyright © 2022
by Sarah Jane Huntington.

CONTENTS

INTRODUCTION

I hope you find, within these pages, stories that you may like and maybe even one you love as much as I do.

The ideas for these strange tales have sat inside my mind for years, desperate to escape. The inspiration came from many places. But mostly, the ideas formed from playing a game with myself and asking... What if? It became my ambition in life to write a book filled with those stories so others could enjoy reading them.

I truly hope they are enjoyed and remembered. Really, I believe that's all any writer craves.

—XXX

DEVIL'S CROSSROADS

Thirteen-year-old Allison's knees cracked and popped as she bent to wrestle a particularly stubborn and spiky weed from the lush grass.

Gardening was her chore for the day, although she never minded it. She preferred weeding to having to wash the windows in the two-story home she lived in, along with her parents and older sister Rachel. She also preferred gardening to being alone in the house with Rachel.

The sun shone hot on her back as she swiped her hair out of her eyes, she glanced up at the windows of her home and wondered if it was safe to go inside for a cool drink. Two thin, long shadows fell in lines across the lawn.

"Snake-oil salesman's in town."

She jumped and squinted. The long shadows belonged to her friends, Jane and Tom. They were standing side by side with wide, matching smiles. Tom brandished a flimsy yellow piece of paper in her face, so close that she couldn't read it.

"Got me a flyer, see," he proudly announced. "Snake-oil man."

Allison rolled her eyes.

"I can't read it that close. Shove it up my nose, why don't you," she laughed.

Jane grinned and winked. She was wearing her second-best dress, the yellow one she sometimes wore to church. Jane was always wearing dresses, she was a sweet, feminine girl who loved flowers and had only just outgrown dolls. She was the opposite in most ways of Allison's tomboy style.

Jane's name was really Elizabeth, but every few months she called herself something different. She switched names according to whichever character she liked best in the books she read. Months before, everyone had been told to call her Emma, before then, she would only answer to Alice.

Allison guessed she'd been reading Jane Eyre again.

"He's parked at Devil crossroads, we can go and spy," Jane wiggled her eyebrows.

"Who is?" She asked.

"The snake-oil man!" Her friends spoke together.

"He's here," Tom added. "He came a few years ago and cured people, my cousin's friend saw him, so it's definitely true."

Allison took the flyer and found herself reading aloud.

"Traveling salesman, for one day only!
Come and see, come and try.
It won't hurt and you won't die...
Cures and remedies for all!
Satisfaction and discretion almost guaranteed.
At Devil's Crossroads, today!"

Allison cackled with laughter. To her, the flyer seemed more like a prank.

"Tell me you don't really believe this!" she said. "Who is he? Snake-oil men were around hundreds of years ago or something. Weren't they? And this is so corny! It's an urban legend or a joke."

"Ah," Tom began. "You might not believe it, but I do, and some folks around here might believe too."

"Yep," Jane added. "Valuable information indeed. If we were to overhear anything good that is..."

Allison looked at her friends, they each seemed excited. They couldn't go to the pool anymore or to the lake, or even go to the park without being bullied by Rachel and her friends. Since they'd all turned thirteen, the bullying had become more vicious and relentless.

They were fast running out of places to hang out together in safety. The older kids Rachel ruled over by fear and by force were all sixteen. They'd taken to throwing empty beer cans at them at the pool and chasing them away. If they were at the park, they would launch stones and rocks. All directed by Rachel as if she were a warlord or military commander.

Allison felt responsible, she'd promised herself she would go wherever her friends wanted to go that summer, just to make up for the trouble her sister caused them.

3

"Okay," she smiled. "I'll get changed. Come inside if you want."

"Is she in?" Tom asked. Allison knew he was referring to her sister, and she nodded unhappily.

"We'll wait on the porch then." He added. "For safety purposes."

She raced inside and changed her jeans and t-shirt after she'd gotten sweaty fighting the weeds, she ran a brush through her short brown hair and crept back downstairs. She knew which creaky steps to avoid by heart.

Near the front door, she held her breath, excited at getting in and out without her older sister knowing.

Two more steps and I'm out, just two more, she thought.

Thunderous footsteps pounded her way.

"Where the hell do you think you're going?" Rachel appeared from the living room with a scowl. "Finish that weeding and do my laundry while you're at it 'cause I ain't doing it."

Allison shut her eyes as her stomach plummeted.

"Tom has a… a… f… f… flyer," she stuttered.

She only struggled with her words when her sister was around, she was so scared of her that she believed her own words were afraid to come out.

"What flyer?" Rachel snapped.

She raised her arm and slapped Allison around the back of her head. She was a large girl and strong too, she pulled on the front door viciously and stepped out.

Jane yelped in surprise.

"Give me that," Racheal ordered Tom. "Before I make you."

"Okay, okay," he replied, and threw his hands up in surrender.

"Get out of here, all of you. Now!" Rachel shouted and stamped back into the house. She knocked Allison to the hallway floor as she sped up the stairs, laughing.

Jane peered wide-eyed around the door as she clambered to her feet, shaken to the core.

"C'mon," Jane whispered, holding out her hand. "Quickly now, before she comes back."

The three ran across the lawn and kept running until they got to the end of the street breathless.

"She is so psychopathetic!" Tom cried. "It's like having a monster in town."

"Psycho what! That's not even a word," Jane answered.

"It is now, it's our word, look she cut me!" He held up his index finger and showed a thin line of blood from a tiny papercut. He started to laugh as the mood lightened a little.

"Allison, you're really going to have to tell your parents," Jane sighed and tutted. For a minute, she sounded much older than her years. "This can't go on, for your own sake."

The three had been friends since they were all five years old. Rachel had bullied Allison from the moment she was born. She believed her sister had been born bad, rotten inside. Every action of hers was violent and every word, malicious or deceitful.

Allison's very first memory was of being pushed out of a chair and the awful pain that followed. Then of being sat in the garden while Rachel launched hard wooden clothes pegs at her head and giggled with wild pleasure every time one struck her.

Over the last couple of years, she'd upped her games of cruelty.

The meanness that she believed lived inside her sister grew with vengeance. Their parents were both oblivious, to them, Rachel was the golden child who could do no wrong.

"They never see it, she's clever at hiding it," Allison explained, "They think the world of her and have high hopes for her future."

"Yeah," Tom spoke, "Because she makes you do her homework and beats you up if you don't."

The trio walked in silence along twisted streets and called at a small store where Tom brought them each a bottle of cold coke.

"Have you read any new comics lately?" Jane asked him.

"No, but I might draw one of the snake-oil man. I wonder what he looks like?"

Tom loved to draw his friends as comic book heroes, and Allison believed he was great at it.

Every winter they would huddle in Jane's house drinking hot chocolate, while Tom acted out comic book stories or explained complicated superhero plots.

"What happened then? When he was last in town?" Jane said.

"Well," Tom began as they walked along. "He pitched up at the same woods, the Devil's crossroads. He was in an old wagon like the ones you see in western movies. He sold remedies and my cousin's friend, let's call him Mike. Anyways, Mike went for a cure."

"For what?" Jane interrupted.

"I dunno, I forgot. He got one anyway and someone else he didn't like got the same problem instead."

"Huh?" Allison said. She twisted the top off her coke, stopping to enjoy the hissing sound. "So he traded his problem?"

"I guess so, everyone in town knew but nobody said anything. I mean, how could they? It was all just a rumor I suppose."

"Weird," Jane said as she linked arms with her friends.

They came upon the treeline to the woods. It was a place they knew older kids with their own cars came to drink and make out. Three separate dirt tracks met up in the middle and local people called it the Devil's crossroads. They all said it was haunted, although nobody ever knew what or who it was supposed to be haunted by.

"We'll cut through," Tom said. "Follow me."

Allison wished she had a sweater, it was cooler inside the woods even though it was a bright hot day. The three crept along like a small commando until they began to hear the sound of a man's deep voice.

"Stay low," Tom told them.

Jane and Allison shuffled along behind him until they came to a thick line of spiky bushes.

A cloth-sided wagon with 'CURE ALL' written on the side stood parked on the exact spot the three tracks crossed. An old grey horse lazily chewed grass at the side of the wagon's small wooden steps.

"Wow!" Jane exclaimed. "This is so weird!"

A very tall elderly man leaned on the wagon's side while he smoked a cigarette. He appeared to be talking to himself or to the horse.

He wore a black suit, a black pair of large sunglasses, and a string tie. On his head sat an old cowboy hat. Allison felt one of her friends yank at her top to sharply pull her down low behind the bushes.

"Someone's coming!" Tom mouthed.

The three crouched down further, each hidden from view as they listened to a car slowly approach.

A red car stopped in front of the wagon and their teacher from school, Mrs. Edwards, stepped out warily. The snake-oil man removed his hat and smiled to reveal black and yellow jagged teeth. His face was gaunt and his cheekbones protruded sharply. His hair was bright white and stood up in wild tufts. He seemed frail and ancient, yet he walked gracefully to greet his visitor.

"He is so creepy!" Jane whispered.

"Another psychopathetic," Tom added.

Allison watched carefully, she didn't dare to breathe as they listened to the secret conversation.

"May I help you, Madam?" The tall man spoke in a deep baritone drawl.

Mrs. Edwards shifted on her feet and kicked at the dirt tracks with her heels.

"I need something for my husband," she spoke shyly.

"Something?" the man asked her.

"Yes, for you know, for the… Well, for the bedroom."

"Ah. I see. Please wait."

The man walked swiftly and disappeared into his wagon. Allison felt stunned and ashamed at listening to such a confession.

"Her husband can't get it up," Tom blurted, and quickly clamped a hand over his mouth.

She felt a burst of laughter rise up and pinched herself to keep it down. Jane stuck her face down her dress to silence her giggles as her shoulders shook.

"No more than one drop per night." They heard the tall man tell their teacher. They caught a glimpse of a pretty yellow bottle tied with a ribbon being handed over.

"How much money did she pay?" Jane whispered, and Allison shrugged in return.

"I can't tell," she hissed.

As soon as their teacher left, another car came from a different direction. Allison recognized the car straight away. It was Mrs. Emerson from the hair salon. She sometimes cut her hair in silence but would talk for hours with her mother, swapping town gossip and recipes.

Mrs. Emerson parked and walked confidently to the man with no hesitation in her steps.

"Hello," she greeted him as if he were an old friend.

"You helped my sister some time ago and I have the very same issue," she said.

The man leaned against his wagon and regarded her quietly.

"I see," he spoke. Without needing to ask for more information, he walked carefully up the steps of the wagon and vanished inside.

"I say, why do you park here?" Mrs. Emerson yelled. "It's awfully isolated."

"Exactly." The snake-oil man replied.

Mrs. Emerson went to open her mouth once more, but stopped herself.

"Boy or girl?" The tall man poked his head out from the wagon.

"Good gracious!" Mrs. Emerson became flustered, she held a hand to her chest as her chin wobbled. "Oh my! Any!"

Allison heard a sigh of pity from Jane and turned from her hidden position.

"It's so unfair. He's a conman," Jane whispered and Tom nodded his head once in agreement.

She didn't feel so sure.

The tall man handed Mrs. Emerson a green bottle filled with shimmering liquid.

"One drop only per night or you'll have a litter," he warned her. Money changed hands, but again, she couldn't see the cost.

As she watched Mrs. Emerson drive away, she could see happy tears fall in a stream down the woman's face.

He sells hope. Cashing in on folks' hopes. But how did he know who Mrs. Emerson's sister was? They don't even look alike.

"We should go," she told the others. She felt knowing other people's secret desires and wishes maybe wouldn't be so useful after all.

"Go where, though?" Jane reminded her and she couldn't think of an answer.

The three stayed where they were, hidden and quiet. They watched as old Mr. Connor from the bakery arrived, he asked for pain relief and left with a pink bottle and a smile.

"Why the crossroads?" Jane spoke aloud. "Because it's isolated, like he said?"

"Magical place," Tom replied. "Like that old blues musician who sold his soul on one so he could be the best and my pa says really he was."

They sat for another hour in silence and threw small sticks at each other.

Allison was intent on landing one on Tom's head when he began to frantically act out motions with his hands. His eyes widened in panic.

"What?" she mouthed. "What's wrong?"

Has he seen us? Is he coming?

Then she heard it. The familiar sound caused her instant dread. Her sister's squeaky bicycle. Their father had offered to fix the squeak multiple times, but Rachel wouldn't allow him. She liked the irritating noise and loved the effect of dread it tended to have on people.

Allison felt her heartbeat thrum in her ears as she realized what Tom meant. A creeping coldness settled over her as Jane realized too, and squeezed her eyes shut.

The situation turned very serious in a single moment. Tom drew a line in the air and held a finger to his lips as the squeaking stopped.

It was vital they stay unseen. If Rachel caught them, that would be it.

She peered through the bushes with one eye. Her sister was standing and glaring at the tall man. He only stared straight back at her, unimpressed by her scowl.

"I want a remedy," she demanded. "Not a cure or a fix."

Allison began to have a sinking feeling.

"I want someone to be sick. As in dead," she continued. The tall man sucked in a deep breath and raised a single white bushy eyebrow.

"Whom do you wish to be dead?" He asked her.

"My sister Allison," she replied without a single hesitation.

I'm going to die. She's going to have me killed.

Jane reached for her hand and held it firmly. Tom patted her shoulder carefully.

"Is your sister horrible to you?" The snake-oil man asked.

"No, she wouldn't dare. I just hate her, okay? I didn't want a sister. I should get the attention. I want her room and her things. She spoils everything. Give me the remedy already!" Rachel kicked at the dirt ground in anger and sent up a spiral of dust.

"Come into the wagon please," he told her.

"No way! You're a weirdo, I'm not going in there with you. Are you a perve or something?"

"Do you want your remedy or not?" The snake-oil man raised his voice so loud that a flurry of birds erupted from a nearby tree.

Tears fell down Allison's face as she tried to absorb the scene playing out before her.

She hates me so much and I didn't even do anything to her!

"Let's go," Tom mouthed and pulled at her arm.

She peered around the edge of the bushes for one last look. She watched as Rachel climbed the steps into the wagon and roughly pulled the curtain across.

The snake-oil man took two steps up the steps and stopped, he turned slightly as his gaze landed straight on her.

He knows we're here. He can see me!

She tensed up and fought the desperate urge to run. The snake-oil man lowered his sunglasses. Impossible bright amber eyes stared out. He winked at her once as a jolt of electricity passed through her.

"C'mon," Jane pulled her.

The three friends ran.

"She's going to have me killed!" Allison cried out as they sped through the woods.

"He's a conman!" Jane yelled.

"I bet it's just sugar water," Tom reassured.

"You don't understand!" She stopped and hit the ground with a heavy sob.

"She wants me dead, she's so horrible!"

Tom and Jane dropped to their knees beside her.

"Come and stay at mine tonight," Jane soothed her. "And I bet Tom's right. It's sugar water. That's all."

"But you said everything came true the last time he was here! Your cousin's friend, remember?"

"Just rumor, local made-up gossip," Tom spoke, waving his hands around in dismissal. "Just like the Devil's Crossroads, it's just a path, that's all. Urban legends and folklore. That's all it is. It's about as true as a comic book."

"Don't worry," Jane soothed her. "Nothing will happen."

Yet Allison did worry. Some curious sense inside her informed her that she needed to worry a whole lot.

The three walked home in silence, peppered with occasional sniffs from Allison. Jane and Tom left for home, with promises to call later, while she went back to her chores. She counted down the minutes until her parents were due home.

It seemed impossible that she should have to be on her guard and consider death at her young age.

I'll watch Mother cook and make sure Rachel doesn't poison my food. At least if I do that she can't slip me a potion. Then I'll barricade my bedroom door tonight and do my best to avoid contact.

But poison could be left on her soap, on her toothbrush, or even in her bed.

She felt such turmoil inside that her thoughts became a black tangle in her mind.

As soon as her parents came home, she offered to help with meal preparations.

Her mother gladly accepted the assistance. By the time they sat down to eat at six, Rachel wasn't home.

"Have you seen your sister?" Her father asked her. She shook her head.

"I bet she's at the library studying, or out with her friends," he smiled. "She's such a good, popular girl."

Allison chose not to answer,

At seven, she went to her room. She dug out her favorite special stationery and wrote goodbye letters to Jane and Tom.

As far as she was concerned, her life was over and she would die at any moment.

At eight, a knock came at her bedroom door.

"Are you sure you don't know where your sister is?" Her mother asked.

"I was with Tom and Jane," Allison told her, so her words weren't really a lie.

At nine, she could hear the mutter of voices downstairs.

She crept onto the landing to listen. The town sheriff stood in the hallway patting her mother on the back.

"I found this flyer in her room, he's taken her," her mother told him. "I just know it." She gave him the yellow paper Rachel had snatched from Tom.

"We'll find her," the sheriff promised, and left. Allison's father left with him.

At ten, she heard her mother crying and dared to venture downstairs. She was sitting alone at the kitchen table with the phone clutched tightly in her hand, her face wet from tears of joy.

"They found her! She must have fallen off her bike. They've taken her to the town doctor. Rachel's okay!"

Allison smiled, not quite sure how to feel. She didn't want to feel relieved, yet she did in a small way. She also felt familiar fear creep back up her spine and deep brutal terror over what might become of her.

She woke the next morning after a mostly sleepless night. For a blissful few seconds, she stretched and enjoyed the sunlight streaming through her curtains. She remembered everything in one frantic moment and sat bolt upright in a panic.

I'll be okay, she told herself. *I'll check all of my food and I won't go near her.*

Wearily, she dressed and headed downstairs. Rachel sat at the kitchen table wearing her pajamas and staring blankly ahead while her parents fussed and made breakfast.

"Good morning," her mother greeted her.

"Morning," she replied and sat. Her mother looked frazzled and on edge while her father frowned deeply. A strange atmosphere hung in the air.

"Rachel, eat your porridge," her father said.

Rachel did, she ate it with careful precision until her bowl was empty.

"Have a drink, Rachel," her mother told her and so she did. She drank a whole glass of milk without spilling a single drop.

"Everything okay?" Allison asked, confused. Her father beckoned her into the living room.

"We found Rachel wandering the crossroads last night. The doctor thinks she might have suffered from a bang to the head falling off her bike. We'll be going for tests. She hasn't spoken yet. She hasn't done anything and she won't unless you tell her to do it. Understand?"

Allison nodded dumbly. While her parents got ready for the hospital appointment, she sat with her sister.

Is this a prank? What's happened to her? She's... empty?

"Are you okay?" She ventured. Rachel continued to stare ahead with glassy, doll-like eyes.

"Lift your right arm, Rachel," she said.

Rachel did, she lifted her arm until Allison had to tell her to put it back down.

She went to the house phone and dialed.

"Jane! I'm so glad you answered! Can you grab Tom and come over? Quickly. You won't believe what happened."

An hour later, the house was empty and the three friends sat in Allison's garden together drinking cold coke while she told them everything that had happened.

"Right," Jane began. "I think the snake-oil man was a vampire, but a kind of energy stealing one or something. I just started reading Dracula. By the way, I want to be called Wilhelmina now."

"I think he's an alien shapeshifter and he's replaced Rachel with another shapeshifter, so be very, very careful. It happened in a comic, so..." Tom explained. "It might be the start of an invasion. We should keep an eye out for more."

Allison considered both of the options carefully.

"What do you think caused it all? A bang to the head like they said?" Wilhelmina asked.

"I think," she started to say. She felt it was important to choose her words very carefully.

"I think the snake oil man was real. I think he took all the evil and meanness out of her, maybe to put in his potions and cures. But, I think because there was so much badness inside her, hardly anything got left behind."

Wilhelmina and Tom gazed off into the distance, both deep in thought.

"He'll come back. One day soon he will and then we'll be able to ask him," she added.

Allison did not add that she also wanted to thank him.

The three friends enjoyed the rest of the summer, much more than they imagined they ever would. News reached them of Mr. and Mrs. Edward's sudden happiness. Mr. Connor became very sprightly and even joined a dance class, and Mrs. Emerson was finally pregnant with triplets and overjoyed.

* * *

Years passed and Rachel remained the same for the rest of her life. No doctor had ever been able to figure out a reason why.

She passed away peacefully in a group home for adults, while painting a picture of a sunflower she had been told to paint.

The snake-oil man never returned to Devil's Crossroads, but there are still those in town who remember him. Every summer, people wait and look for the familiar yellow flyers to appear, desperate for a personal remedy that they know will change their lives.

PAINTED BLACK

Nina sang along to the music playing on the car stereo, happily oblivious to her out-of-tune vocals as Max drove and concentrated with a deep frown.

"Shhhh," he hissed, and turned the stereo off. "I'm a bit lost, I need to think."

"I was enjoying that!" Nina complained. "I love to sing along, and how can you be lost when you grew up here?"

Why do people always turn the stereo off when they're lost? She thought.

The pair followed twisted country roads in Max's old rattling car, slowly creeping around each bend with apprehension and worry over hidden ice.

"It's changed a bit, the hedges have been cut," Max remarked as he squinted at the road. "And I think we should have turned left."

Nina sighed heavily. She'd been looking forward to seeing how beautiful the Derbyshire countryside would look in the heavy snow of winter, but the novelty of the white scenery had worn off after the first hour. Max had told her the drive would take two hours roughly, but it had already been double that. She longed to stretch her legs and breathe in the clear, fresh air.

"Everything does look the same," she admitted. Thick bushes lined the crumbling bumpy roads while flat, desolate fields stretched in each direction. Only the occasional cluster of snow-covered trees broke up the eye-watering monotony.

"Wait, here we are," Max smiled with relief. Nina craned her neck as the bushes parted, revealing a long gravel driveway.

"Ours is the first house in the village, the rest are that way," he nodded further along the road.

A two-story cream-colored cottage stood waiting, Nina gasped sharply at the sight. Thick smoke poured from the chimney and each window was decorated with pretty, dark wooden shutters.

"It's beautiful!" She cried in surprise. An abandoned pond stood at the entrance surrounded by old statues and figures covered in moss. Max circled and parked. He stared blankly at the house for a few long seconds before he turned to Nina.

"Are you ready to meet them?" He asked.

Nina felt a ripple of nervousness. For the whole journey, she'd been excited to meet Max's parents and now she felt wary. They'd only been together for four months and she'd quickly found herself in Farthing village, in the middle of nowhere in the thick of winter.

They were set to stay for three days and she hoped time wouldn't drag or be too awful. She checked her phone and saw there was no service.

"I'm a bit nervous now," she admitted. "Hey, have you got a signal?"

"Nope, you won't get one around here, come on. You'll be fine, they'll love you."

Nina stepped as gracefully as possible out of the car, she felt a blast of cold as her lungs burned in the crisp cold air.

It really is gorgeous here, she thought. She knew Max had grown up in Farthing town and hadn't left until he was twenty. They lived close to each other in the city and met at their local pub. They'd fallen into a relationship quickly, more quickly than Nina had felt ready for.

They crunched their way across the gravel as the main door of the house opened with a resounding creak. A tall older man stood in the doorway, dressed in a thick blue knitted jumper and smart trousers. He smiled broadly as Nina saw the resemblance to Max straight away.

"Dad!" Max shouted, and the two embraced. A tiny lady with delicate features and short white hair stepped out from behind them. "Mum!" Max said and hugged her, while Nina stood smiling and waiting.

"This is Nina," he finally announced.

"Come in dear, I'm Max's mum Maisie, this here is my better half Tom."

Maisie held out her hand warmly and Nina took it. "I'll make tea, come and sit," she told her.

Tom patted her firmly on the back several times until she flinched, "Welcome to our village and welcome to the family."

"Oh," Nina said and felt her eyes well up with tears. He led her to the sitting room, while Max disappeared to fetch their luggage.

The room was decorated with family photos in pretty ornate frames. Each one featured Tom, Maisie, Max, and his sister Lisa, who had died at age fifteen. Max always refused to talk about her.

A small dusty television sat in the corner and cozy blankets draped lazily over comfortable, wide sofas. To Nina, the room felt wonderful and homely. She took a seat as Tom sat opposite her.

"Max told us you're from London originally?" He asked, crossing his legs and peering at her intently.

"I am, yes, but it was too busy. Frantic, really. I moved to Derby to be near my brother but he… well, he died in a car accident last year," Nina replied, swallowing the lump in her throat.

"Ah, sorry. We've had our losses too, our daughter. Do you have any other family? In London perhaps?"

"No, unfortunately not. But I have plenty of good friends and now Max, of course." Nina tried to smile widely to lift the mood.

Tom seemed very solemn to her. He nodded his head and looked deep in thought. He met her eyes and blinked rapidly.

"Do you live alone? A roommate perhaps?" Tom asked.

"I um…no, it's just me."

This is a bit strange.

"And work? What is it you do again? Proofreading Max said?"

"Yes, that's right," Nina spoke, feeling as if she were in a job interview.

"In an office or from home?" Tom queried.

"Freelance, so from home."

Why is he asking such weird questions?

She began to feel uncomfortable.

Max appeared in the doorway and joined them.

"I hope my dad isn't asking you a thousand questions and being weird," he teased.

"Not at all," Nina lied. "Shall I go and help your mum with the tea?"

Max and Tom stared at each other, neither one blinked. They reminded her of two cats meeting. She excused herself and left the room.

She could hear Maisie bustling around in the kitchen, she followed the sound along the hallway and saw her gathering biscuits to place on pretty china saucers. Steam poured from a flowery kitsch teapot.

"There you are, love," Maisie said, louder than necessary. "Carry this for me, would you, dear?"

"You have a beautiful home," Nina told her, taking hold of a heavy tray.

"Thank you, very kind of you. Come along now," Maisie ordered, and walked carefully along the hallway. She stopped abruptly by the living room door and swung around. Nina almost crashed into her and gasped. Maisie's glassy blue eyes locked onto Nina as her smile dropped.

"Run," she hissed almost silently.

"What!"

Maisie turned away, she arranged her face into a smile as Nina stood stunned.

* * *

Nina wrapped her coat tightly around her small frame and stepped out of the house. It had taken her almost two hours to get Max alone to ask him if he would show her the village. In those hours, her mind had spun in circles while her stomach had bubbled with anxiety. She'd caught Maisie's eyes a few times, but the woman had acted politely and simply smiled at her while Nina drank cup after cup of bitter tea.

"What do you think of them?" Max immediately asked, wrapping a scarf around his neck.

She took a deep steadying breath, "Listen, can we leave? I feel…"

"What! No! We just got here. Why would we leave?" He interrupted.

He waved to his parents who watched them from the window with smiles plastered on their lined faces.

"Your mum said something odd. She told me to run. I can take your keys and leave, I'll drive back in a few days and fetch you. I just want to go."

Max stopped and glared at her, wide-eyed and tense. He opened his mouth to speak, but paused. She watched as a range of emotions played out across his face, the anger drained out of him and emptiness took its place.

"My mum has dementia. I should have told you, but I thought you might not come here."

"Oh," Nina said, deflated. "So she's just confused?"

"Probably yes, she says things that make no sense sometimes. She doesn't realize that and the doctors can't do anything."

The two walked in silence towards the village, both lost in their own thoughts.

Nina reached for Max's hand and squeezed.

"I'm really sorry. I understand, and it wouldn't have stopped me coming here, you know. I like her, I like them both. You could have just told me. I was so worried!" She said.

"Thanks. I should have. Take anything she says with a pinch of salt. Let's have a quick drink, yeah?"

Nina nodded and saw two rows of smart houses lined up opposite each other. The village shop stood in the middle of one row, with a simple weather-worn box painted black outside. On the opposite side exactly, stood a tiny pub called 'The Feast.'

"This was a mining town for years, but the mines closed down in the eighties. Almost everyone left," Max explained. "My dad was a foreman at the big mine, about half a mile from our house, just across the road."

"Wow," Nina breathed, "How many people live here now?"

"Twenty-seven."

"Are you guessing? How could you possibly know exactly?" She laughed.

Max shrugged and led her towards the pub.

Inside felt toasty and warm, only one older man sat at a small table by himself, reading a thick book with an old sheepdog sleeping by his feet. He glanced up and nodded.

"This is nice, cozy," she remarked, and took a seat by the window. For Nina, the pub felt more like being in someone's home. She wondered if it had actually been a house until the village found itself in desperate need of a place to drink.

She gazed out of the window and watched as fresh flakes of snow gently spiraled to the ground. A woman close to her own age walked swiftly down the road with grim determination. Nina stared as she posted a yellow piece of card into the black box. She tucked her head down low and walked quickly away.

What's that box for? A postbox? But they're red, not black.

She looked at Max, he was deep in conversation with a man behind the tiny bar, heads close together and muttering. Nina watched as a bent-over elderly man passed the woman outside. He tipped his woolen cap to her and approached the box. He, too, slid a yellow piece of card into the slot.

"What's that box for?" Nina asked as soon as Max sat down.

Without a glance at what she was staring at, he spoke, "It's a postbox, of course."

"Right," Nina's voice dripped with sarcasm. "Some kind of weird village tradition. Black postboxes, It's been painted black Max."

"This isn't a weird village, Nina. Good people live here."

He placed a glass of white wine in front of her.

"I don't doubt that. But why is it black? Aren't they meant to be red by law?"

Max chose to ignore her.

I really don't like this place.

Something about the whole place gave her deep unease.

She watched as a small car pulled up to the box and a tall man, too big for the car he drove, climbed out. Dressed in a suit with shiny, freshly polished shoes, he walked confidently to the black box.

He removed an ornate silver key from a chain around his neck, opened the back of the box, and picked up a stack of yellow cards. He tucked them casually into his jacket and turned to the window directly at Nina, he locked on to her eyes and winked once.

"Who's he?" she asked.

"Nobody really, just the local mayor."

"Tiny villages have mayors?"

"This one does. Drink up. It's almost dark."

"Max, why are you acting strange?"

"I'm not acting strange, you ask too many questions."

"So does your dad," she said.

Max slowly shook his head.

Nina felt a sudden curious feeling, she wanted to do what Maisie told her, she wanted to run. A brief thought crossed her mind of stealing Max's car keys and of driving as fast as she could and never coming back.

There's something off about this place. Something feels very wrong. Mayors and weird painted post boxes, it looked more like a ballot box. Is this town even on a map?

She sipped her drink deliberately and slowly under Max's watchful eyes. *Do I trust him?* She questioned herself, *Yes, I suppose I do. Don't I? But it's only been a few months.*

She drank the rest of her wine and pulled her coat on.

"That tasted awful," she whispered. "Cheap."

"Mum and Dad are making a roast, so I hope you're hungry," Max said and waved goodbye to the barman. "They'll have good wine."

Nina knew it wasn't a long walk back, but she braced herself for the cold and looked behind her to see her own fresh footprints in the snow.

"So pretty," she whispered, unaware that she was slurring her words. The two walked back the way they'd come. Nina stopped as a sudden wave of dizziness spread over her. Sweat broke out across her back as her legs began to wobble.

"Max," she stuttered in confusion, "Something…is…"

Her vision swam as she fell onto the short pavement with a painful thud. The last image she saw was Max's face inches from her own before crippling blackness overcame her.

"I'm sorry," he told her. "You need to know that, I'm sorry."

* * *

She awoke to thick crushing darkness pressing down endlessly, she curled herself into a ball and wondered why she felt so freezing cold and heavy. She shivered deeply. Her mouth felt dry and sore and her lips were cracked. Her thoughts slipped away from her as she tried to stretch and felt her whole body ache.

Where am I? Did I have an accident?

She tried to remember where she'd been. A jolt of fear spiked through her as her memories flooded back.

Max! What did he do to me? Think, think! Did he drug me? The wine? Where am I?

Wild panic sparked and started a fire inside her. She forced herself to breathe slowly.

Calm down, I'll be okay. There must be an explanation.

She wriggled each finger, testing them in turn, then began on each of her toes. The ground felt hard and damp underneath her. She tried to sit up as she realized her feet and wrists were bound. Brutal pure panic tore through her. Nina began to gasp and whimper as she struggled.

"Don't fight it," a voice spoke, the sound echoed and bounced dully.

"Who's there? Where am I?" she croaked.

"I'm Harry and you're in the mines."

"What? Oh my God."

Don't lose it, you'll be fine. Don't panic. Breathe, just breathe.

She took ten deep lungfuls of damp air as the smell of sulfur hit her senses.

Whatever's happened, I can get out of it. Stay calm and think.

"Can you move Harry?" She finally whispered. "Did Max do this?"

"Can move, but there's no point," he said.

"Are you tied up?"

"Nope, no way out, and I ain't even gonna try."

Nina squinted as hard as she could and a shape began to form, heaped up against the rock wall opposite her.

"Why are we in the mines?" she asked, afraid to know the answer.

Thick silence filled the air. Nina's mind felt full of static.

"That bloody thing we feed. My name's on the paper this year," Harry coughed and wheezed.

"I don't understand," she pleaded as a sob escaped.

A few moments passed and Nina began to pick at the bindings around her ankles. Her wrists were tied at her front.

Duct tape? It's loose!

She rummaged around on the ground for something sharp, anything that might slice the binds, but her tied hands came up empty.

"No harm in telling you the truth, I suppose," Harry said. "You may as well know why it is you'll be dying soon."

Nina felt a jolt of terror at the man's words. She forced her arms into painful positions to check her coat pockets and found them empty.

"Tell me then," she said and went back to searching the ground. Her hand landed on a palm-sized solid object. She grabbed it and began to slice.

"Started in the sixties, it did. They disturbed something in these mines. Woke it up, I reckon, or let it loose. It needs to eat every winter. Kids were lost, whole families gone. They fed it hikers sometimes or folk just wandering through. Campers and such. But no one comes nowadays, especially not in winter. So, they started a ballot. Votes. Two gone every year. Your fella, he's been fetching a young lady every time, a handsome man like him has no trouble finding 'em."

How could I have been so stupid!? Fight this, get out of here. I'll kill him. That fucking idiot.

A quiet rage, a dangerous rage, threatened to overflow her. Her stomach churned, she gritted her teeth and continued to slice.

"That's it? You all just fucking feed it. You don't think to leave and get help? You just murder people instead. It's crap. You're lying. Everyone's insane here."

"Eh now! It's not as easy as it sounds. Farthing's our home and with it being here, well, our crops grow strong. We make a lot of money, lass. Hundreds or more years ago, folk did the same. Think about it. They sacrificed virgins or warriors to feed a beast, a dragon, or some such underground thing. Folklore's full of them tales and legends. It's always happened, and it still does. It's just hidden now. Our beast is ancient. Ain't poorly understood superstition and we ain't mad."

"This is crazy! Shit like this doesn't happen in real life. Some psycho in your village is doing this. It's Max, isn't it?"

"Not so," Harry answered. "I assure you. I've seen it. Many times. It's always been going on, always will. Max is a cog in a wheel and now't more."

"Then I hope it takes its sweet time eating you. You're all mad," Nina spat.

Harry laughed bitterly.

"You never wondered why people disappear from all over? They're food, I tell you. Food for something else. They live underground."

"Shut up," she hissed.

She fought the urge to scream, everything Harry said sounded absurd to her. It was something from a horror movie or a fairy tale.

In the distance, she heard a muffled roar of fury.

What is that? This can't be happening! Do they really think some kind of monster lives down here? Crazy. They're all crazy.

She began to slice rapidly.

Nina was strong in body and mind. She could be fast and quick when she needed to be. She knew she would not go down without the absolute fight of her life.

"Where's the way out, Harry?" She called.

"You won't escape, don't even try. No one gets out. It's coming, lass."

"You think I'm going to sit here like a fucking idiot? Waiting for this cult bullshit you all believe! Who tied me? They were as pathetic as your story, Harry."

"It's not a story! Quit fighting."

Nina growled and pulled at the wrapping around her ankles, the sudden release and break of the tape sent her sprawling backward painfully.

NOW MOVE! Her mind screamed.

She scrambled up and felt the wall nearest to her, moss and water covered its surface as she groped her way along.

If there's a way in, there's a way out. Someone had to dump us in here and leave.

"STOP, just stop alright!" Harry's yell echoed as Nina cringed.

"I lied. I lied all right. We hold it back. We feed it to hold it back! Not for crops, but for the good of others."

Nina ignored his words and concentrated. Her hands fought to find a doorway, a hinge, or a handle, anything that might mean a way out. Her heartbeat thudded in her ears and almost drowned out any other sound. The ground began to vibrate behind her in thick, heavy thuds.

"Please," Harry wailed. "You don't understand. We're a sacrifice. We hold it back. We've got to hold it back! We ain't the villains' lass. We ain't!"

"Fuck you," Nina screamed.

Her hands hit an opening in the pitch black as her fear spiked, her legs turned to rubber and her bladder gave out in fright.

She hauled herself up into the hole as a deep guttural growl filled the mine. The hairs on her neck stood up as she crawled and shuffled inch by inch with difficulty. Her mind imagined thick strong hands grabbing her feet and she sobbed with terror.

It's a tunnel, I'm in a tunnel.

As soon as the knowledge popped into her head, she heard a deafening scream of agony. Snarling and tearing sounds filled the air as Harry's cries turned to gurgles.

Nina frantically crawled and dragged herself, small nails and sharp objects tore into her, ripping her coat and skin. She barely felt the pain. She tumbled out the other side and landed on the white snow-covered ground. She lay breathless, panting, and crying.

You're out! It's someone dressed up in there, some sicko or Max himself.

The moon illuminated the scene as if by design, she looked around cautiously and found herself alone in a woodland clearing, the mines at her back. Pitiful metal fencing barricaded an opening, along with warnings of danger and trespassing signs. She squealed as she opened her hand and found her sharp object looked to be a piece of bone.

"Fucking freaks!" She spat and threw it deep into the woods.

She sat up, then shakily stood, bright red blood dripping down onto the fresh snow.

They just dumped me here and left me to die. How could anyone do that!? That lying bastard!

Nina felt rage, a primal fury of the kind she'd never felt before. Her instinct had warned her about Max several times, and yet she'd ignored her feelings.

Can he get out? Whoever it is, can they get out?

An idea began to occur to her as more adrenaline flooded her system. She took a deep breath and kicked at the metal fencing, she pounded and thumped until it became loose. She picked up the biggest rock she could carry and pounded again until one single panel fell, crashing down with a heavy, deafening clang.

"COME AND GET ME!" she screamed into the mine. "I'm not afraid of you."

It's a person, it's a mad person.

A person was something she could deal with. A person was someone she would stand a chance against.

Nina threw her coat down on the ground and ran. She raced through twisted trees and jumped over fallen logs, desperately looking for the road and the path that led into the village. Her lungs burned, her wounds bled, and her head thudded. Determination flooded her system. Vengeance filled her mind.

She saw lights in the distance. She stopped to take off her jumper and dropped it, she ran harder. At each moment, she felt sure someone was behind her, about to reach out a monstrous arm to grab her.

The familiar house stood out, lit up by its warm, luring glow inside. Nina ran across the gravel, not daring to look behind her. She balled up her fist and pounded on the door.

She rested her head briefly against the thick wood as the door flew open. Tom, wide-eyed, stared at her in shock.

"Nina, h…how did you…" He babbled. His expression was one of immediate fear.

Nina barged past him, intent on one thing only. Max ran out of the living room shouting words she couldn't absorb as she dived for his jacket. Grabbing it, she ran back outside. She fumbled in the pockets with shaking hands until she had the car keys.

"Nina, Nina!" Max shouted. "What's happening?"

Tom, Maisie, and Max stood in their doorway, each one of their pale faces full of fright.

"You picked the wrong damn woman this time! You crazy bunch of cult bastards!" She yelled.

"Nina, please. STOP! Listen to me!" Max pleaded. "Is it coming?"

"Fuck you," she spat.

Nina slid the car key into the door and climbed in. She yanked the door shut and hit the locks with seconds to spare.

"He followed me," she whispered. As she had hoped he would. Except, it was not a human. Not one bit.

A large creature crept slowly up the driveway, massive paws the size of dinner plates crunched down on the gravel. Its entire body was covered in filthy, matted and bloody fur. Glowing eyes of yellow locked onto the house as it snarled, while thick drool dripped from its pointed, bloody teeth.

Its ears stood upright as it took powerful, yet gentle, strides.

Wolf? Nina thought absurdly, knowing it was twice the size of any wolf she'd ever heard of. It reared up on muscular hind legs, revealing a blood-splattered chest as it shrieked and wailed a high-pitched sound. Long razor-sharp claws uncurled as it landed back on all fours with a heavy thud.

"Impossible," she whispered.

She watched from the safety of the car as Max pushed his parents inside and slammed the door.

The creature sniffed the air and drew back sharply. A thick, long tongue whipped at the cold air, snake-like in its movement.

In one brutal leap, the beast smashed straight through the cottage window, diving inside. Screams of fright and pain pierced the night. Nina hunkered down low and clamped her hands over her ears. Tears poured down her face as she tried to block out the ripping, snarling, and howling sounds of agony.

She waited. Not daring to move, she sat and shivered, curled up in the footwell of the car. She finally heard the crunch of gravel recede and prayed the creature was making its way towards the village.

She straightened up.

Should I check if anyone's alive?

"No," she told herself. "Fuck them."

She started the car and drove. Blood dripped down her face and she let it.

Nina drove past a *You are now leaving Farthing* sign.

"Fuck you, fucker, and your fucking village. Fuck you all!" She raged.

As soon as she was clear of the sign, she turned the radio on. A happy, upbeat song rang out as more snow began to fall.

Nina laughed a manic laugh and began to sing along.

She did not see what was coming up behind her.

The creature hit the side of the car in one massive impact. Nina twisted and turned as the car rolled over and over until it landed in a ditch. She groaned loudly, barely conscious.

What the hell just happened? What did I hit? Another car?

She found herself upside down, the seat belt dug firmly across her chest. White-hot agony engulfed her head as blood dripped slowly down. Her breath came out in ragged wheezes. The pain in her ribs felt like fire.

She heard deep growls from outside, the sound overtook the frantic beating of her heart. Thick thuds hit the bottom of the upside-down car as the creature jumped.

Nina screamed in terror.

I've let it out! Harry wasn't lying. I've let it out. I'm going to die, was her last coherent thought.

The huge muscular arm of the beast yanked her kicking and screaming out of the car. She passed out as her body was torn and ripped apart. The creature ate greedily, a vicious hunger without limits.

It padded its way towards the next point of light, the next village, and beyond.

THE VOID

Now

Kate cuts a lonely figure as she stumbles towards the ramshackle slanted house that sits both bravely and defiantly alone. A crooked home in a mirror world, one of obscure shadows and grim emptiness. A reverse, a shade, a memory, a ripple in a pond of former vibrancy. The edge of the Void.

Her body feels weighed down, impossibly heavy, and crude.

In the distance, on the highest jagged hill within sight, a cluster of shapes wandered along its spine. To Kate, they resemble paper cut-out figures, each linked closely together, hands joined, heads down low.

Silently, she steps forward up the twisting spiral path. For her, there is no point in making the journey into the burning city. Not anymore. Now she knows hope itself has died its own inelegant death.

The house is abandoned, of course, she can feel its emptiness and hunger for company in her soul. Black moss grows up the side of the small house and rotten Ivy trails along the roof, a relentless takeover by nature, or some twisted version of it.

Kate pushes at the half-decayed door. It creaks eerily, but doesn't resist her touch. Furniture lays in ruins inside, scattered toys and broken dishes.

All discarded in the owner's rush to leave, she supposes. But still, only a remnant, a haze, a dead season.

"Hello?" she instinctively calls out anyway. Her voice is muffled, underwater, hardly a sound.

She explores the small home to make sure it's empty of any form of life before she claims it as her own. Kate finds nothing but bare room after bare room.

Each one is stripped down to its most basic core of a damp rotten mattress and stained floor.

Outside, she hears the frantic flapping of a boat's rotten sails caught in the wind, she knows the sound has a secret meaning, wings. Thick, leathery wings that belong to a wicked flying beast.

She hears frantic whispers, gently at first. A small suggestion of noise, until quickly, her sanctuary is surrounded.

Kate cannot remain unseen, she holds her hands over her ears and throws herself down into the nearest corner. Thick cobwebs touch her skin, her hair, her mouth. She screams silently at the invasion.

She clamps a hand over her mouth, fuelled by instinct, and freezes. For a few beats, the only sound is her frantic heartbeat thundering in her ears.

How can my heart still beat? She thinks. *It's broken, after all.*

"Let it be quick," she whispers. "Please God, let it be quick."

Kate knows that if God exists, then He or She cannot hear her plea. Not here, not now. God appears to be absent.

A single tear falls down her cold cheek as she shivers. The will to live, to survive, seeps out of her like blood. The whispers sense the change and prepare to feast.

Kate always liked to imagine she had a chair in her head. A small wooden one in which she used to sit. She conjures up the idea now, in her mind she sits and watches her happy memories play on a screen set out in front of her simple chair.

She sees one of her parents, from years before, a replay stored inside her brain and recorded without her knowledge.

She sees Jack, perfect Jack, until her own mind betrays her too.

His face alters without her meaning to change it, to the last moment she saw him. His features turn afraid, riddled with deceit, infected by association.

She sees his strong hands, blood-covered traitor hands.

In the absence of a realm without a creator, she thinks and has no idea why. *The absence of life in the abhorrent. Not a void. It was never a void.*

The whispers descend. The noise becomes deafening in its fury. The sound of her own screams muffles the chaos. Fear breeds anger, deep inside.

Kate yearns for blackness, for emptiness. For what might come after the after is finished.

She no longer feels the agony, the pain, the terror, the ripping and tearing apart. Anger grows. With it births a triumph. Fire burns and sparks erupt. Embers pour from her body. The blinding clarity of color in a gray world. A transformation.

Revenge is her last coherent thought.

Then

Kate watches with interest from the highest, most lonely pew of the auditorium as her professor's voice lulls his students into a steady sleep. His mild German accent has sent each one of his Parapsychology students, except for her, into an almost hypnotic state.

Outside, a steady stream of rain falls. A single flash of lightning explodes, turning the dark blue sky white for a short, barely there second. The flash makes an intricate pattern on the back of her eyelids.

Now count, Kate reminds herself. She counts to eight seconds before a rumble of thunder makes itself known. *Sixteen miles away? Or is it eight miles?*

She finds she can't remember if the seconds should double or not.

A quick glance around tells her she's the only student still paying attention, she leans forward to hear over the sounds of the storm.

"Frequency changes or vibrations of atoms themselves is my theory. Among others," the professor chuckles.

He peers over his half-moon glasses at his dreaming crowd.

"It is my belief that upon death, a vibration occurs, a frequency change. A soul, for lack of a better term, is released and freed into another realm. Now, raise a hand if you're still here or rather, still aware," he smiles.

Kate raises her hand and waves until the professor's old and humble eyes notice her.

"May I ask a question?" She half shouts.

Two students mumble and tut at her, yelling.

"Certainly."

"Other realms, other dimensions. Is there any proof they exist? Scientific proof I mean?"

The professor taps his pen thoughtfully. He begins to gather his papers and pauses.

"Experiments are ongoing, I believe. But the current suggestion agreed upon is eleven. Eleven dimensions outside of our visual range. We see so little of what exists on the spectrum of visible light. Less than two percent, in fact. Think of it as tuning a radio. Other stations play, but our metaphorical dial can only be set to one."

"Could we change our dials, in theory?" Kate asks.

"I don't believe we should, but perhaps save that question for a philosophy class young lady, the esoteric is not discussed here. You should know that. Class dismissed."

The students below Kate spring to life in a mass exodus of shuffling and bag collecting. Almost all of them will be leaving for Thanksgiving, all but Kate.

She shrugs into her old, saggy, and still damp coat. She wraps the itchy wool firmly around her. She grabs her beaten-up leather satchel and walks down the few steps toward the professor.

Kate wishes to know more, she yearns for it. The beginnings of questions tumble around in her mind. The professor sees her, and she knows that he sees her. He chooses to pretend he hasn't and walks swiftly out of the private exit, the one meant for staff only. He locks it behind him. Kate stops in her tracks, feeling more hurt than she can explain to herself.

I'm invisible. Completely invisible.

She waits on the steps until the sounds of happy voices outside the room become distant. She listens to the whoops of joy and feels a stabbing sensation in her heart.

Everyone is going home, except for me.

Kate cannot go home. Ever again. Home for her is a distant memory she should have savored, but failed to. Head down, she leaves and walks as if her only destination is an electric chair or gallows. Other students rush past her, some crash straight into her, and still, no one sees her. No one notices.

Kate has been a student at Willinger college for almost a year. Within that time, she has made no friends. Nor has she tried.

Only the fierce collection of girls, three of them, pay her any attention, and not the good kind.

She darts out of the way of whole groups chatting excitedly as she crosses the small quad. The rain pours down and stings her eyes.

Willinger's dormitory is almost empty as she yanks at the door and stamps her feet on the worn-out mat. All the lights are on brightly, yet somehow, to Kate, it still feels dark. No matter how many lights she uses, it is always too dark for her.

The small lounge the students use is empty, Kate pauses and wonders if she should sit by the fire while no one is around and try to get warm. A flurry of footsteps racing down the stairs changes her mind.

The three girls come down as Kate steps back, half-hidden by a bundle of coats hanging on a rack. The scent of expensive perfume and hairspray follows them.

The girls rule the college unofficially, although everyone accepts their reign as fact. They are the ones who get to decide who becomes popular and who is cast down from their circle. They shine their charismatic lights on the few and sneer at the rest. Papers and homework are done for them, by others wanting in on the clique, as they paint their nails, gossip, plot, and plan. Cruelty lives inside each one, a deep vileness passed and shared from girl to girl.

Kate despises them with a passion. As soon as she'd stepped foot on the campus, they'd hated her too. Kate with her pretty dark hair, her elfin looks, and her silent mystery. Her refusal to talk or to attempt to join their group, her denial of their existence and power.

The three girls gather in the lounge, bickering and sounding to Kate like a cluster of chickens. She makes a break for the stairs and takes two at a time until she's clear.

"Hey, weirdo!" One calls after her. Kate pulls at the door at the top of the stairs and vanishes into the hallway.

"She's a disgusting freak!" She hears one shout. The harsh words ricochet around her mind.

A few doors are open as she walks along, head down, determined to get to her room unseen. Different rooms play different music. Rap songs meet her ears, then pop, followed by classical, played by some high-brow student.

"Hey!" she hears and smacks into a warm chest.

She gasps and stops, takes a step back, and sees Jack.

"You okay Kate?" He asks.

Kate sometimes believes she's in love with Jack. He's the only person in the entire college that ever made any effort to speak to her. He's also the token boyfriend of one of the three girls.

"I'm fine," she says. "Have a good Thanksgiving."

"Do you want to get a coffee?" He asks.

"I... No. Sorry. I can't... I..."

Kate tries to smile but her mouth is dry, sandpaper raw. Her lips stick to her teeth and her smile becomes a grimace. She scuttles away with her cheeks burning.

Her room is the last one along the never-ending corridor. She fumbles in her bag for her keys, fighting her panic.

Sweat breaks out across her back even though she shivers. Finally, she unlocks the door and slams it behind her. She throws herself on her unmade bed and sobs.

She thinks of Jack, of how he and everyone else go through life as if they were a tiny duckling. All of them have complete trust in those around them, they swim and paddle together in life, not worrying or caring about what might lay beneath them in the murky water they swim in.

Kate does worry. She knows what hides in the dark water. She knows exactly what lies waiting. She knows the kind of thing that might reach up and grab. She's seen it before.

Kate has secrets. She keeps them locked in a wooden chest, padlocked and chained inside her mind. Those secrets chase her and snap at her heels, no matter how fast she tries to run.

She wakes to complete silence. Darkness has fallen and the moon sits fat and shines like a spotlight in the night sky.

Am I here or there? She thinks.

She tests her fingers, lifts them one by one, and then starts on her toes. She can't tell. She feels weighed down, not light.

She stretches and feels a tingle. It starts in her belly, warm at first, and it spreads. Kate gives in to the familiar feeling. She's come to enjoy the sensation over the years.

At first, she felt nothing but panic and terror. Now, a pleasure takes hold, freedom like no other. The hot tingle spreads and turns into a shimmer of electricity. Her skin hums with power as she lifts. She is a mist, a spiraling gray mist. A silver cord that glitters, caught in the moonlight, tethers her to her body. Her body becomes an anchor, the cord her chain as she floats towards the ceiling.

Kate thinks of the professor, she thinks of his clever atom theory and vibrations, the radio stations. She can change her dial, her metaphorical tuning fork, and she can do so with ease.

A surge of euphoria erupts inside her as she passes through the ceiling, up through the tired old attic jammed full of broken furniture, and out. Out into the night. Kate cannot feel the biting cold as she glides. She cannot feel the sad looks she has become accustomed to, the degrading stares, the disgust, and hatred. The revulsion.

She floats along as if swimming over the empty campus, over the few remaining cars. Over the quad with its old benches, over the treetops, the thick bushes. She twirls and spins, lost in her own out-of-body dance.

Her cord yanks, preventing her from traveling further. She touches her belly in wonder, at least, the place where her belly should be. She grabs her tether and pulls, she works her way back.

A flapping monstrosity flies above, busy with its own needs and desires. Kate has seen them before, she doesn't fear them, they pay her no attention. She wonders if they can even see her.

Two lights in the dormitory blare like beacons in the dark night. Kate cannot resist. She dives towards the light as if she is nothing more than a moth to a flame. She hovers and peers.

The curtains are open in one room. Posters and cliche quotes about love decorate the walls. Jack sits on a lush double bed, surrounded by fluffy pillows. He is bare-chested and, to Kate, beautiful. His skin gleams. One of the three girls, the one named Kerry-Anne, lays naked between the soft sheets. Her hair spirals out behind her and she touches Jack with hands that should be Kate's.

She cannot hear what they say to each other, although she can imagine. Kate feels a burning in her heart, a fire starting up all of its own accord. She pushes away from the wall and heads to the next lit room. The other two girls, part of the three, sit cross-legged on a bed. The bed has stuffed animals lined all in a row and a pretty satin cover, the girls play cards and smile at each other the way lovers do.

One reaches to touch the other's hair, a delicate caress. They kiss, a deep kiss full of illicit passion. Kate realizes she knows the secrets of others as well as her own and that it is not just her who has stayed behind after all.

Her cord judders, a warning. It begins to turn hot in her hands. She follows the shortening tether back to her room. Back through the window, back to her body. She settles back inside herself like a pair of comfortably worn pajamas.

Kate opens her eyes, her bodily eyes, and smiles.

The next morning, she feels famished. As if she hadn't eaten for days. She tries to recall if that's true or not and realizes it probably is. She wonders where she can get food from.

The vending machine? Steal from the empty unstaffed kitchen?

The idea of finding someone else's food to eat propels her from her bed. She collects all the change she can find and scampers down the stairs. She is afraid to come across the three girls. Kate wants to remain hidden and invisible until everyone is back. Safety in numbers, anonymity in a crowd.

She makes it to the kitchen, fills her metallic flask with stolen coffee, and takes a tub of cheese sandwiches. She finds potato chips and chocolate in the vending machine and counts out her coins to buy them.

"I didn't know you were here. Freak," a nasal voice speaks from behind her.

Kate jumps and tries hard not to react. She knows the voice, she feels the tone crack her insides wide open.

"Nobody at home wants you? Can't say I blame them."

Kerry-Anne stands at the foot of the stairs with her hand on the acorn carving of the banister. She looks and behaves as if she is the queen of the manor, which Kate supposes she is. She has pretty blue eyes that like to peer into the business and lives of others.

"I'm studying," Kate mumbles.

"Ha! It speaks."

Jack appears abruptly, he looks at the two women, eyes back and forth like a tennis match.

"Hi Kate, you're not leaving?" He asks.

"Her family doesn't want her, nobody does," Kerry-Anne laughs. "She got dumped here, I saw her family speed off in relief."

"Leave her be Kerry, she doesn't bother anyone."

"She bothers me," Kerry-Anne hisses. "The freak."

Kate feels her heart thud at Jack defending her. Her cheeks fill with fire.

"Kate, we'll all be in the lounge tonight. Just a smoke and a drink with a few friends. You can join us," he says.

Kerry-Anne's blue eyes widen and she blinks rapidly with heavily kohled eyes. A snarl crosses her pretty, perfect features, a challenge, a dare, "Yes, join us. What fun that'll be." Her voice drips with sarcasm.

"No, thank you," Kate replies.

She turns back to the vending machine and pops the coins in, trying to distract herself.

"Come on Jack, there's a bad smell in here," she hears Kerry-Anne say. Jack tuts but all the same, shrugs and follows his girlfriend. The two argue in heavy whispers.

The queen is displeased.

Kate leans her head on the cool machine, suddenly desperate to lock herself in her room. She can sense chaos coming, almost as if the scent of imminent horror itself is in the air.

She leaves her chocolate laying abandoned in the machine and runs, racing back to her room.

She slams the door behind her and tries to catch her breath.

I hate it here, I hate it so much and everyone hates me.

For the hundredth time, she thinks about leaving. She thinks about running and finding a solitary life within a crowd of strangers. She thinks about going home and remembers she can't.

My family is afraid of me. I can't go home, they hate me too.

Kate slides down the door and lands in a tangle on the cheap plain carpet. She wishes she were nothing. She wishes she were dead, although she knows full well that there is no such thing.

* * *

At age seven, Kate learned to fly.

"I can fly all the way up to the stars," she told her parents. They grinned at her and nodded, happy to play along. "Of course you can, sweetheart," they smiled and rolled their eyes.

At age ten, Kate had proudly told her babysitter, Mary, that she could see her in her bedroom while she slept. "How nice," Mary told her, laughing along with the childish game.

"It's true," Kate said. "You have a pink bedcover and a poster of New Kids on the Block, you have a cream dresser and red nail varnish is spilled on the surface. Your dog Willow can see me."

Mary stopped babysitting.

At age thirteen, Kate told her mother that her father sneaked out of the house to visit the woman down the street late at night and she knew what they did.

Her father left.

At fourteen, she woke her mother in the night to tell her that Grandmother was lying on her own kitchen floor dead. Her mother ran the two blocks to her grandmother's house, let herself in, and found her body stone-cold dead on the kitchen floor.

Kate was sent to boarding school. Kate was sent to college.

Kate was not allowed home.

She had no real idea of why she could travel out of her body or how. For Kate, shedding her earthly self had become as routine as taking off her clothes at the end of the day. She did not believe she died each night, she did not wake up exhausted each morning, only hungry. She did not entirely know where she traveled to. She only knew it was the same world in daily life that she explored, only… it was different, too. She called it the Void, although the name never quite fit. A reflection, an inversion, a shadow world, a gray ripple of the real world. A place that defied reality with pleasure.

On occasion, she'd seen others. Blobs of darker grey prowled the landscape, clumsy stick figures walking along as if they'd stepped straight out of a child's drawing.

Kate even saw a clockwork dog once, absurdly chasing its own mechanical tail. Spiderwebs hung in trees, thick webbing as thick as rope. Fires burned in empty cities and once, rain fell that she could feel.

Ancient winged beasts roamed the skies, while the odd human-shaped figures wandered back and forth endlessly.

The Void was the home of many oddities. Kate sometimes felt the shadow world was a place between places. A gap stuck or formed in the middle of separate layers of real worlds. A landscape of mistakes or a world for those who slipped through the cracks.

The world without, the world of the Void, is the one Kate craves to belong in.

* * *

She stands and crosses to her desk, eats her stolen sandwich, and switches her computer on. She checks her email while she chews thoughtfully. Nothing. No happy Thanksgiving messages. She switches the machine off and gazes outside instead. She watches the drip of gentle rain until it starts to pour. Kate wants a shower, but she doesn't dare risk running into the three girls.

I smell, I need a shower. They'll all be downstairs, it's fine, I'll be fine.

Decision made, she scrambles for fresh clothes. She finds some flannel pajamas and grabs her dressing gown and towel before she lets herself change her mind.

The shared bathroom is six doors down, she counts them off and touches each door for luck as she passes.

Her ritual works, the bathroom is empty. She chooses a stall and turns the water on. She only has soap, but someone has left a bottle of shampoo. She takes a bit, even though she knows she shouldn't. The smell of apple and mango hits her as she froths up her hair. The water feels glorious on her cold skin as she washes. For the first time in days, she feels warm.

She catches sight of a blonde head as she turns the shower off and wraps herself in her towel.

Which one is she? She thinks. She knows the head belongs to one of the three girls, but she can't decide which.

Kate forces her wet arms into her gown, intent on leaving and getting dressed in her room.

"I didn't know anyone else stayed," the girl's husky voice says. "Oh, it's you."

Amber, Kate remembers and conjures her name, she's the prettiest one of the three. One of the two girls she'd seen kissing last night.

"I'm studying," Kate says.

"Okay, cool. Whatever."

Amber stares at herself in the steamy mirror and leans forward to apply more lipstick. She has a jaded, tired look that Kate finds unsettling, she wonders if she has it too.

"It's okay, you know, to be whoever you want to be," Kate whispers.

As soon as the words fly out, she regrets it. She forgets she doesn't know how to speak to others correctly. She forgets that people are repelled by her, forgets that she should stay silent. Her stomach drops as her pulse quickens, acid collects in her throat.

"What are you talking about?" Amber hisses, the huskiness turns to a growl.

"Nothing… I… I saw you and… her. No, forget it."

"Saw me and who? What are you trying to accuse me of?"

"Nothing."

"Have you been spying on us!? Kerry-Anne is right, you are a freak."

Amber spits the last word out and takes a threatening step toward her.

"Stay away from us. Seriously." Amber jabs her hard in the chest.

"Sorry," Kate whispers, her cheeks aflame.

"Kerry-Anne hates you, we all do," Amber seethes. "It's about time you got what you deserve."

Kate feels cold all over again, she yanks at the door and runs back to her room. She feels for her keys and unlocks the door. Her hands are shaking.

I'm useless, I'm absolutely useless. I'm never leaving this room again! Why did I say anything?

She climbs into her bed and covers herself. More than anything else, she wants to sleep. She wants to leave her body and explore the only world she feels safe in.

Kate doesn't realize she's left her door unlocked, with her keys on the outside for all to see.

Within an hour, she is deeply asleep. At least, her body is. Another part of her begins to rise. Her ascent this time is quick. Intention and need are her fuel as she lifts up, up out into the starry sky. For the first time, Kate wonders if the stars are the same in the Void world as the Earthly realm. She tries to remember the patterns, shapes, and twists of the pinprick lights so she can compare the two constellations.

She feels her tether pull, it jolts her and sends her whirling backward as if it were an elastic cord. She feels as if she is an astronaut on a spacewalk.

Below her, thick gray swirls cluster in the car park. To Kate, up high, they resemble inkblots.

She ignores them and speeds away, she twists and twirls, somersaults, and whoops with silent joy.

Freedom, true freedom, she thinks. She wonders how she can think, with no physical brain. She laughs in exhilaration and wonders what her professor would say if he were to see her now.

The lounge lights in the dormitory glow, they pull at Kate to investigate but she resists the urge, ignores it. She plummets in a dive, holding out her misty arms. She slams on imaginary brakes and stops. She is hung ghost-like over the spiderweb-covered car.

I hope I never see what makes those.

In the distance, a new sound. One she has never heard inside the Void before. Whispers. The calm, soothing sound of secrets whispered between lovers. Kate glances around and spins. Her strange world appears empty.

The lounge light pulls her again, a soft pull of apprehension. She glides over and places her misty hand on the steamy old window.

The room appears empty at first. Discarded beer cans lay on the wooden floor, throws and blankets are scattered around. A single graceful feminine calf and foot pokes out from the worn sofa. Kate has the urge to knock on the window.

Would anyone even hear me?

For her own amusement, she knocks. Her misty fist makes contact with the glass, but there is no sound. Not even a dull underwater thud.

Before Kate has time to think about that, the window fills with Jack. She gasps and jolts back. Her heart aches when she sees that he looks upset. He closes his eyes briefly and lowers his head. He speaks words Kate cannot hear. Feels emotions Kate cannot touch. He raises his arms to close the too-thin curtains and she sees. Blood. Blood-stains all over his hands.

Alarm rattles through her. A shiver races through her ghostly form.

Is he hurt?

Kate spins, unsure of what to do. Through the haze of the curtains, she sees Kerry-Anne, strutting peacock-like into the room. She throws her beautiful head back in a throaty laugh. She stumbles, drunk, high, euphoric. Amber follows with her graceful dancer's walk. The jaded look has left her, in its place is madness, anger, passion, and triumph.

Kate turns bitter cold, an emptiness takes a hold of her. It starts in her heart and spreads out in thick tendrils. Quick and complete desperation. She looks down at her stomach, her cord has lost its shimmer. Powder falls from it as if disintegration has set in, even rot.

Panic overwhelms her. She swoops inside, up the stairs, and along the endless hallway. She knows. She feels it with every atom of her being.

She passes through the wall and sees her sleeping body. No, not sleeping. Her small body lies as if dreaming. A pillow, her favorite pink one, sits on top of her face. Stab wounds cover her chest, four holes. Four betrayals. Her tether falls away completely. Lost, gone.

"WHY?" she screams silently.

Why would they do this to me?

She lays discarded as if she were an unwanted doll. Abandoned. Dead. Murdered.

A weight settles in, her lightness leaves her. Her mist takes form, human form. Solid, gray, a shadow with texture. Kate tries to run, she hits her closed door. Trapped, stuck, solid, imprisoned.

She cries but she isn't heard. She wails but she isn't noticed. She pulls at the door and runs, still unseen by those around her. Her feet slap on the hard cold floor and out. Running still, broken inside. She looks for a place to hide, a place to think. A place to curl up and scream.

Now

The descending whispers recede. Challenged by Kate's fury, they jerk back in one hive-minded fast motion. Black passion grows inside, the rips of her soul remain, the holes gape open. Still, she stands. A scream of rage jerks her body. Her anger is a force, a growing power.

Her needs and wants become focused. Swirls of whispers circle her, like a school of fish, waiting, watching.

She screams again. This time, the sound travels far. Kate is heard. Her mind sees images, flickers of faces. Enemies, foes, adversaries, nemesis.

Three girls, she thinks. She cannot recall who they are or why she should feel such brutal hate, only that she does.

Kate cannot feel anything else outside of vengeance.

Her heavy body becomes lighter, the solid meat and flesh of her bones fall like ash. Kate becomes a mist. She knows the feeling, a familiar soft glove.

Whispers recede, each scatters and hides like fallen marbles.

Despair, revenge, justice. She craves destruction. A shimmer of blue light, a pulse, the only color in the grey world, forms in her chest.

Kate remembers.

Her heart feels beaten, her mind a labyrinth, her spirit battered, her soul twisted. Swirls of patterns whirlwind around her, a darkness forms at the edges. A blade of black pierces her, pulls her apart, and reorganizes in a moment.

Kate remembers she can fly. Memories flood her, and her wooden chest of secrets opens wide. She lifts. She leaves the abandoned house, it was never her prison, her place to hide after all. She rockets towards a bleak unnatural sky, she sees white, the purest whitest light she has ever seen. She stops.

No. No. No. NO!

She plummets down, down, down until the surface of the ground readies itself to swallow. She freezes, she swoops, she searches. She finds.

The campus, her campus. A dollhouse of stone. Her traitorous pretend home.

The site of her death, the culprits inside. One glow of light sparkles, it shines like a lighthouse, a signal just for her. She dashes forward.

Straight through the window, an arrow streaking out from the curtains. Kate finds herself in the student lounge. She stops, she waits as a tangle of black rage spirals around her.

Jack sits by the fire, half his face is lit by a warm orange glow. He stares at the flames, deep in concentration.

Kerry-Anne dances. Her hands run smoothly over her body as she moves to music only she can hear. She opens one eye to check if she's being watched by Jack, or by her friends.

Amber watches her cat-like from the sofa. Her eyes are narrowed in interest. In her hand is an almost empty bottle of vodka.

Lisa sits shivering, wrapped in a blanket, a thick joint between her shaking fingers.

No one senses the change in the room, the sudden chill, the sudden scent of the other.

"We're going to prison," Lisa states abruptly.

All eyes land on her. To Kate, their voices are echoed, far away, muffled.

"All we do is say we didn't see a thing. We were all down here. Together. I'll report a prowler later. I'll do it now!" Kerry-Anne laughs, alone. The sound is stubbornly tinny.

"I can't lie," Jack says. "You killed her."

He jabs a finger at Kerry-Anne and Amber. "You two, you're sick. I hate you. I'm not covering this up."

"Darling, if you don't do as I say. You'll lose your scholarship, fail a drug test too. Your daddy will beat you black and blue. Again," Kerry-Anne sings. "You made more of a mess trying to revive her!"

"She was a bitch, a nasty freak!. She knew things. Things she shouldn't!" Amber yells and starts to laugh wildly while Lisa cries.

Jack stands and puffs out his chest. He starts to speak but his mouth opens and closes, silent, a fish without air.

Feelings are the language of the soul, Kate thinks.

The conversation in front of her dulls. A hissing sound starts up in her ears, anger brimming to the boil. A black-hot frenzy bubbles, a crescendo of wrath. Static fills her mind.

Kate screams a high-pitched scream. One made purely from rage.

The people in her sight, with their evil and selfishness that flourishes inside, become her target of fury.

Kate jerks towards the four of them. Amber senses her, but too late. Kate focuses her revenge into her fist until her misty self takes solid form.

She punches Amber's chest. She feels skin and tissue separate as easily as butter. She feels bones crack and open. She feels the hum and beat of a warm heart. She pulls, yanks.

She holds the stolen heart high as if she's won a bloody, gruesome trophy and roars. Amber's eyes open impossibly wide and cloud over. She sways back, her vodka bottle falls and rolls lazily away. Kerry-Anne shrieks. She throws her manicured hands up to her face in horror.

Now it is Kate who laughs. The mirror over the fireplace wavers and shatters. The sound seems like a thousand tortured screams sent straight from hell itself.

Shards of sharpness pierce faces and bodies. Lisa screeches and throws herself onto the floor. Kerry-Anne chokes. A blade of glass sticks out of her delicate neck. Blood trickles as she holds it in place.

Kate grips the end and tugs it jaggedly across her throat. Blood spurts out in a flood, a gurgle, a fountain, a river of warm life seeping away. Kerry-Anne's face cracks apart like an old and broken porcelain doll.

"Murderer," Kate whispers as Kerry-Anne falls. She feels certain she's been heard this time, seen and heard.

Kate turns to Jack. To his pale and milk-white terrified face. A dark spot stains his jeans at the front, his shaking legs betray him as he falls to his knees.

"Please God, please," he says.

Kate feels sure that God has nothing to do with it. Her darkness spirals and twists around her, she is engulfed by brutal pure hate. There is no place for redemption in her mind. No corner in which hope or pity might lurk. Only the clarity of fury.

She has become something more.

Kate's ghost-like fingers stroke his face gently, a bitter caress. She runs her hand down to his throat and squeezes. The power inside her shatters his windpipe, crushes bone and cartilage, and severs nerves in one ruthless swipe. Jack falls face down, his beautiful features quickly turn blue.

One remains.

She turns to Lisa. The girl tries to stand, tries to run, to flee, to leave.

"I didn't do anything!" She screams.

Kate yanks her hair and halts her in place. Her hand reaches inside her skull and finds warmth, the center of being. There is no resistance when she pulls, her temporary form feels stickiness, feels life. Lisa's scream penetrates her mind until she screams in return.

Four bodies lay in various tangles. Four dead betrayers. Murderers and accomplices all.

A stillness settles over Kate, a silence. She thinks of her body, and without meaning to move, finds herself transported to her single room, gazing down at her former self.

For a small moment, she feels a pang of sadness. For her, the world was always too dark, no matter how many lights she used.

She knows that no one will miss her. No tears will be shed for her. She repelled others, those who sensed she walked in two worlds.

Her death will be nothing more than an inconvenience. She resigns herself to the fact that maybe in death, people will talk kindly about her, more kindly than they ever did in her short life.

Kate remembers she can fly.

She floats up, slowly at first, until she flies at speed. With no tether, she can explore the world she inhabits. She can watch the burning cities, explore and feel unafraid if the whispers draw near. She can find others, ones who slipped through the gaps. Others that don't belong in her world. Her world is for oddities, the discarded, the broken, and rejected. The Void is for her.

She turns, spins to see her last view of the campus. She sees four figures crowded and huddled near the main door. Lost, broken, punished, frightened souls. She can smell their despair, taste their fear.

Kate laughs a gentle laugh. She will send the whispers and the blacker than black inkblots their way. She will lead the flying things directly to them.

She pushes on. She thinks of her cord, her anchor. It was a chain that bound. She is lighter than light. She is glad.

She is free.

SURVIVORS

Lucy pads back and forth across the dirt-covered floor of the cabin in her already worn out and filthy socks. She stops occasionally, listening to the sounds of outside filtering in through the tiny cracks in the thick wooden walls.

Birds, she thinks, *As long as I can still hear the birds, I'm safe?*

Anxiety floods her system. She picks and chews at her already jagged and varnished pink nails. The tired remains of a manicure she'd had especially for the trip.

She couldn't have guessed that the pretty cabin she'd chosen online would become her prison. Their prison.

A rustic location of blissful and private solitude, the laminated brochure she'd sent off for had promised. Lucy had jumped at the chance, a whole week for her and Adam to reconnect after drifting so disastrously far apart.

* * *

"I've been seeing someone else," Adam had told her after she'd found his credit card receipt for a hotel. A cheap dive of a place, perfect for sordid affairs with cliche willing secretaries. Lucy hadn't guessed, she hadn't even suspected, and the betrayal had torn her apart.

He always had been expert level when it came to the telling of lies. Lucy believed she was the one person he would always tell the truth to. He had promised such a thing in his wedding vows, after all. Another lie, no doubt.

The cabin trip had been an expensive treat to try and save their marriage. A costly adventure she'd hoped would pay off more than the initial grimaces and challenges she'd faced. The first was persuading Adam to take a trip and then how to pay for it.

"Waste of money," her cheating husband frowned. "Why do we need to go to the middle of nowhere? When we can stay home and argue instead."

But she'd insisted, demanded, eventually begged. Yet the stubbornness Adam despised in her, the trait he always said was a weakness, had ended up saving both their lives.

* * *

Lucy steps close to the window, holding her breath and peering out through the too-thin curtains. There are no movements that she can see. Outside stands a small dirt yard littered with a few old tools. Their old car sits parked up at one side, like an abandoned toy, discarded and useless. A thick line of trees stands guard, an open gap in the middle breaking apart for a dirt path. The path winds through dense chilly woodland and leads to a large and pretty boating lake.

They explored on their first day, walking the path all the way in silence to the shimmering water.

Lucy had wanted to jump in, simply so she could feel something other than the deep hurt raging inside her. She hadn't jumped. Adam had stopped her. The loud alerts on his cell phone had started right at that very moment.

Lucy closes her eyes and prays. She has never been the praying type, yet over the last few days, she has begged God for help more than she ever has in her entire thirty-four-year life.

She imagined the trip might mean the end of her marriage, not the end of the world.

Abruptly, the birds stop singing and leave the trees in a mass exodus of frantic flapping.

Lucy doesn't hesitate, she drops to the floor and quickly scrambles to her pre-arranged place behind the old soft couch. She tucks her head down as low as she can and fights off the terror.

What's happening? Are those things here? Is someone else out there? Don't answer the door, no matter what, she tells herself.

Those were Adams' words too, the last ones he spoke before he left a whole day ago. He'd closed the door firmly with an expression of despair written on his face and left, armed with an old crowbar they'd found and his backpack. Gone to search for food and supplies.

Lucy tries to calm her breathing while her heartbeat drums relentlessly in her ears.

A scraping sound from outside makes her jolt, as sweat drips down her back. She has never felt so afraid in her life.

This is it. They're here. I'm going to die.

She squeezes her eyes shut tightly and tries to think of happy memories. One of her riding a bike for the first time in front of her proud parents. Their joyful faces and smiles before she veered off and fell.

A memory of her wedding day she chooses to push aside and thought of her giggling happily with her group of friends in a bar.

Where are they all now? Are they dead already? Or trapped and hiding too?

Lucy can't help herself, hot tears fall as a loud sob escapes her lips.

She reaches up to clamp a hand over her mouth and bites down on her finger painfully. Her stomach plummets as she realizes she's probably given herself away. A single thud sounds on the roof. Icy terror creeps up her spine as she starts to shake.

If they find her, she wants her death to be quick.

She listens as hard as she can, waiting for more thumps, imagining the sound to be the heavy footsteps of an unimaginable monster.

If they see me, I'm dead.

* * *

"We need to hide, Lucy. They can only see you when you move," Adam had told her. "The news stations all report the same thing."

His cell phone had died then, minutes after the first alerts. The generator the cabin ran on had died moments later and they were left completely in the dark.

"A whole city looked destroyed, Lucy," Adam said. "I saw footage of these massive things swooping down and snatching people from the ground."

"What things?" She'd cried, engulfed by a panic so strong she'd wanted to run outside screaming until the monsters themselves came.

Adam had shaken his head and stared solemnly into the distance, "Creatures. Things come from somewhere else."

"Where?" she'd pitifully cried, "I don't understand! Come from where?"

* * *

Lucy stops listening, she clamps her hands over her ears and gently hums to herself. *I'm so tired. I want a hot bath and clean sheets. I want to sleep and forget this ever happened.* Tears drip down between her feet, making a puddle of sadness on the wooden floor.

I want to rewind time. To before. I should have stopped Adam from leaving. What if he never comes back? What if all I can do is wait to die?

She is exhausted. Stress, panic, adrenaline, shock. If she could only close her eyes and escape her situation.

She wakes. Her neck feels sore and tender. Her eyes widen as she realizes she fell asleep.

"I'm safe, I'm okay," she croaks to herself.

Her legs cramp painfully, but she doesn't dare to move. Not yet. Instead, she listens. *No birds, but it's nighttime. Can those things see movements in the dark too? And what was the thud? Trees?*

While she slept a dreamless sleep, the cabin turned pitch black and she blinks rapidly to try to focus her eyes on the darkness.

She tilts her head to listen harder, all she can hear is the thrumming silence of the night and her frantic heartbeat.

"Move," she orders herself. She remembers there's still a bottle of water in the kitchen and it's at least half full. She crawls slowly over on her hands and knees, aware of her joints popping and crackling. She pauses to wait with each movement, just like Adam showed her, until she reaches the bottle in relief.

An almost silent scratch on the barricaded front door makes her spit the water out and cough deeply. She freezes, desperate to cough more, and clutches at her chest. She hears a quiet knocking in a familiar practiced pattern.

"Lucy," she barely hears.

It's Adam! He made it!

She stands up, feeling her joints snap in protest as she races to the door. She drags a small chest of drawers across, the scraping sound reverberates loudly around the cabin as she winces.

She flings the door open wide as Adam half falls through, landing on all fours.

"Shhh," He whispers, eyes wide and frightened. "Don't move. I think they're out there."

Lucy peers into the darkness and waits. The moon is out and the stars are shining.

"I think it's okay," she tells him.

The pair crawl across the room to wait in silence in their places behind the couch. Lucy stares at a canvas print that hangs slanted on the wall, a scene of a beautiful flowery meadow drenched in hot sunlight. She wonders if she'll ever see anything like that again.

Why didn't I appreciate it while I could?

When Adam decides it's safe, he raises his hand.

"What happened?" This is the first thing Lucy wants to know.

"It's hell out there. Dead bodies are lying everywhere on the roads and those things are eating people. They just snatch people and fly away. Gone."

"What do they look like?" Lucy whispers in horror.

"Awful, monstrous flying things," he says and shakes his head, unwilling to speak further.

"Tell me." Lucy asks, "What's our plan? We can't stay here."

"No plan and yes we can because we don't have a choice," Adam snaps.

"But the Police, the Army. We must be fighting back?"

Where are the jets? Or the Military? They wouldn't just leave people to die? It can't be worldwide, that's impossible, isn't it?

"Maybe somewhere they're fighting, but no one can fight out here."

"Adam, if we hadn't come here, we might have been dead already."

She tries to hold Adams's hand, but he pulls away sharply as tears slide down her face. She can't imagine what it must have been like for him. Having to leave her behind while he risked his life for food. If he thinks it isn't safe to leave, then they have to stay put.

Help will come. It has to.

"Okay," she sighs.

Adam shrugs and, in slow puppet-like movements, fetches his pack. He holds up a few tins of soup and chocolate bars like trophies and manages a brief smile. Lucy nods gratefully as he lays down on the sofa, a sigh of exhaustion escapes his lips as he rolls himself into a tight ball.

"I'll keep watch," Lucy tells him. "You sleep."

She settles into a hard chair by the main cabin window and gazes out into the night.

Next time, I'll go out for food, I can do it. I'll stay low and careful and I'll leave when it's dark.

She wonders what it might be like to see people snatched clean away and carried off and what it might feel like to come across dead bodies lying abandoned on the ground.

Wait, it can't be both? How can people be snatched and still be laying in the streets? That doesn't make any sense.

Lucy holds her hand to her forehead as a swell of panic erupts inside her. Once her thoughts latch on, she can't unravel the idea or stop the flood that inevitably follows. She starts to think of the day she found the credit card receipt.

The way her stomach dropped to the floor in shock, the way cold numbness spread through her body until she couldn't stop shaking. She thinks of how she put the pieces together and checked every single date. The nights Adam claimed to be out with friends from work, he was in a hotel instead. She thinks of the lies he so easily told her. The betrayals, all done without an ounce of guilt on his conscience. When she'd confronted him, he'd been more upset about being caught out and confronted.

I don't trust him. I don't even know him anymore. Coming here was a stupid mistake.

But if people were snatched away, there wouldn't be bodies on the ground. Think, why would he say that?

Lucy thinks of what she's witnessed of the creatures firsthand. She thinks of what she's experienced for herself. Nothing. She only has Adams' words to go on. He told her everything he'd seen on the news and only he saw and read the alerts. Only he witnessed those creatures. Only he has been outside the cabin since it started. His phone had died before she could see anything for herself.

An awful thought begins to spiral out of control as Lucy follows the thread.

This can't be right? He wouldn't, would he? What reason would he have? Does he really hate me that much? Does he want to make me go mad? Or kill me from fright?

She thinks about all the arguing between them.

The fighting first started a few months ago. Adam's words, his anger, and his final brutal decision. The threat that had hung over her since.

"I don't want you anymore, I want a divorce."

She begins to pace while the feeling of claustrophobia takes a firm hold of her. She pulls at the neckline of her old jumper, fighting the suffocating feeling. It feels to her as if the walls are closing in to crush her.

He wouldn't. I'm just tired. That's all it is. I'm tired and afraid. I'm not thinking straight. Am I? It's just paranoia, isn't it?

"No, no, no," she silently chants to herself.

She tiptoes to the kitchen and rummages around in a drawer. When the alerts first came, Adam had taken her own almost dead phone away.

"I'll keep hold of it, I don't trust you not to use it. There's only enough power for one call. If that, we might need it," he'd told her.

Lucy had agreed, he was right. If she had it, she would have called her parents the first chance she had and drained the dying battery. But she knows where he put it, she saw.

Her hand finds the familiar shape and she gently brings her phone up close. It feels lighter than it should and she holds it out into the light the moon casts down. The battery is missing. Lucy silently replaces it. She shuts her eyes tightly, then turns to the sink and vomits.

I'm being set up. Gaslighted. That's what it's called. He wants me to go mad. Or he wants me dead.

She slides down the cupboard onto the cool floor. A manic laugh escapes her and she pushes her face down inside her jumper. A blinding thought occurs to her.

I should kill him first.

She stands back up and rummages once more. Searching through the cutlery drawers. Her hand clasps a large steak knife and she brings it out, holding it close to her chest.

Just in case. She is reassured by the weapon.

Lucy creeps across the wooden floor and stands over Adam sleeping, she resists the urge to wake him up and ask him. She wants to challenge him and tell him her suspicions. She wants to see his expression, but she knows he'll only argue back and deny everything. Besides, he lies so well that his words appear to be the truth.

She toys with the idea of holding the knife to his throat and making him tell her.

If it's all a lie, the world is fine, there are no monsters, no dead bodies. Adam is the monster and he can't know that I know.

She starts to shake as she feels hot bile rise, she swallows it back down scorching her throat. Quietly, Lucy sits down and stares blankly out of the window. A calm fury begins to twist her thoughts further.

There's nothing bad out there, the bad is only in here.

As soon as the first light of day leaks into the sky. Lucy throws open the front door, the door she was never ever supposed to open.

She runs and doesn't look back. She has a plan.

She races along the trail that leads to the lake, jumping over branches and gulping deep breaths of fresh air until her lungs burn in protest. She remembers that other cabins are dotted around the shoreline of the lake. She plans on going to each one and knocking until she can find someone to help her, someone who can call the police and save her.

My husband, she practices in her mind, *he's trying to make me insane or kill me. Help me!*

Lucy knows she looks half-crazed. Her clothes are filthy and she smells. Her hair is greasy, her eyes are red, and she's exhausted. She's certain now that the things, the creatures Adam says are real, don't exist at all.

She breaks through the treeline and spots the water, a bubble of hope rises in her chest and she almost laughs.

Lucy expects to see boats or people milling around. Hikers getting ready to walk or campers in tents clustered around having breakfast.

Those are not the sights she finds.

She skids to a halt and freezes. A gasp of shock bursts out of her mouth as her legs give out underneath her. She falls, crashing to her knees in despair. She is unable to comprehend exactly what it is she's looking at and her mind begins to quickly unravel.

Four bright blood-red eyes, all set in a single line, stare. All four belong to the same creature that stops eating to gaze at her. It tilts its oval head to one side curiously. Two vertical slits open in its face to sniff the air deeply.

The creature is the size of a two-story house. It rears up on thick dry scaled hind legs as Lucy feels her bladder give out. Its chest is covered in light-colored, blood-soaked fur.

A vast mouth opens widely as it bellows louder than a ship's foghorn, revealing layer after layer of yellowed teeth as big as elephant tusks and a long pink wet forked tongue.

Thick translucent vein threaded wings flap out powerfully behind it as it hisses.

She screams in desperation and horror as she sees that the thing it was eating used to be a human. She tries to shuffle backward, sobbing loudly, but in seconds the creature takes two massive strides toward her. The ground vibrates under its muscular weight.

I'm sorry Adam, I'm so sorry.

She doesn't move, but it can still see her. It blinks its many eyes and she can see herself grotesquely reflected in each one like a circus mirror. With a vicious, deep-throated growl, it lunges and grabs her around her waist with its mouth. It lifts her high into the air above the trees as jagged, sharp teeth rip into her.

"Lucy!" she hears Adam shout her name over her screams.

She hits out at the creature's head with her fists, uselessly. She blacks out and falls limp as white-hot agony tears through. Her screaming ends. The creature raises one of its two deadly claw-ended arms and pulls her legs, ripping her in half with a fierce twist and shower of hot blood. It devours and discards, gulping whole chunks, eager for more.

It raises its head in triumph and roars an ancient cry into the creature-filled sky. A thousand other hungry roars return its call.

THE HOUSE AND I

I don't recall when it was that I first lost myself.

Maybe it was long ago, back in the beginning, or perhaps it was somewhere in the middle. No one can ever remember the middle of anything. The beginning or the ending, almost everyone can recall those parts. Or should I start with the first time I saw the house, I wonder?

That could be the moment when my mind truly began to slip and fray away at the edges. At the very least, it's where the careless stitches holding me together first came undone.

The house itself was perfect to look at. A vast and ruthless, cold beauty isolated in the countryside, simply because it would put any other homes near it to shame.

Nothing around it could compete with that enigmatic presence it held. Not even the pretty roses the gardener planted dared to bloom near. The effect made the land seem barren, only I sensed the truth that no life was brazen enough to challenge the house.

The house was vibrant, a manor, and it caught any passing admirer in its playful gaze. It was the plush dominant cat and the people inside became the little frightened mice against its relentless and beautiful power.

I stood enthralled for five or more minutes, or it may have been hours. I was staring and thinking and feeling riddled with self-doubt. The curse that had plagued my own life reared its brutal head, and I'd hastily taken a step back before I caught myself.

I stopped and closed my eyes tightly, I breathed in the warmth of the last bits of autumn sunshine and briefly listened to songs of the pretty birds hidden in thick and almost naked trees.

The house called me, I felt it whisper my name gently, eagerly. Its force and energy tickled my skin until I felt the static pull at my skirt.

We were the same, the house and I.

Both neglected, misunderstood, and yet still harsh and soft simultaneously.

I walked forward, slowly at first, until I burst into an ungraceful run.

Time is fickle, it ticks by too quickly if you let it, or too slowly if you pay too much attention. Time plays with memories, our minds recall events in the wrong order. At least, mine does. Time and regret belong together, hand in hand, like lovers wandering lonely streets in the thick cold of winter.

I should have run the other way. But I couldn't. As soon as my eyes landed on that home, I belonged to it and it to me. Running would never have changed that.

My job was supposed to be a simple one. I was to catalog everything of value inside and discard everything that was not. The instructions had worried me from the start. After all, who was I to decide the worth of anything?

I was cheaper than an official curator in that I would work for free and I was willing to live alone for three months in the house. I was also meant to clean. I was to scrub the house from top to toe, although it lacked toes entirely, of course.

The moment I turned the ornate pretty key in the heavy oak door, I felt at peace. An emotion I'd failed to experience in years. Tranquility overcame me, coupled with bliss, and I smiled broadly. I clutched my stomach in anticipation of the butterflies that were about to take flight inside me as I pushed the heavy oak door wide open.

A soft burgundy carpet greeted me while a shining banister snaked its way elegantly upstairs. The last of the sunlight picked up the dust in the air until it looked like tiny orbs were drifting softly in a galaxy of their own design and creation.

I could smell fresh bread, although I knew that was impossible. The house had stood empty for months, I knew that. The door swung shut behind me and I hadn't even realized I stepped inside.

Home, my mind whispered. *You're home Anna.*

I set my suitcase down and shrugged off my coat. I slipped my heels off and felt the immense freedom and relief in being apart from the absurd shoes that made up the clothing, the costume I wore.

First things first, I decided, tea. The kitchen was modern, with stainless steel surfaces that gave it a cold, clinical feel. The gunmetal colors felt unnatural, an imposter room in an extraordinary house. I tested the power was on, pleased to find it working. I filled a kettle that was likely more expensive than my entire wardrobe and prepared myself to explore.

"Upstairs first?" I asked myself aloud.

I acted as if it were Christmas morning and I'd been gifted the whole house. I ventured into each room respectfully, at first, until I couldn't help myself. I bounced on beds, single ones, and a glorious regal four-poster one that I knew would be mine. I opened wardrobes and brought the clothes inside up to my face. I touched and smelt, caressed, and embraced every item. I ran my fingertips over every surface and not once did I grimace at the thick dust.

I only felt a steely determination to bring the house back to the beautiful glory it deserved.

The bathroom had a claw-footed tub. I squealed with delight at the discovery, I couldn't wait to have a bath and to feel the hot water embrace me. For many years, I was only ever able to have showers.

A single door stood at the end of a long landing, I pulled and yanked until it gave in and opened. An attic greeted me, one full of broken furniture, cracked mirrors, and porthole windows.

I raced back downstairs, giddy with excitement at more rooms to explore. The main living was lined wall to wall with thick dusty leather-bound books and expensive wooden furniture. I had the curious sensation of having been miniaturized and popped into an antique doll's house mansion.

A pale wooden door stood soldier-like at the end of the living room and I opened it with a flourish. Boxes. It contained row after row of boxes, each one had a number handwritten on its side. I assumed they were the items I had to value.

A second sitting room contained pretty decorative plates with matching cups and saucers, all kept locked away in glass cabinets. Portraits hung on the walls, paintings of elegant beauties, and portly, happy men. The room adjoining was stacked high with boxes too.

I opened one and found stamps kept precisely in leather folders. Another had a remarkably old teddy bear with one glassy eye stuffed inside. A big wooden chest held jewelry in smaller boxes, they each played music as a tiny figure span in circles.

"You're forever stuck," I whispered to the ballerina. I knew how she must feel.

Don't think about it all now, Anna, I warned myself. *I have three months. Three whole wonderful months. Don't think about him.*

I fetched my tea and rummaged for biscuits. I noticed a stack of notebooks and a single pen on the side with a carefully balanced note placed on top.

I opened it greedily and read aloud.

"Dear Anna, please make yourself at home. The housekeeper has filled the cupboards with food, also the fridge, and the freezer. Enclosed is fifty pounds, should you need it. Any issues, please call Mary, her phone number is included. We will meet you on our return by which time you will have cataloged and priced my father's belongings."

I crossed the room and opened the fridge. As promised, it was jammed full of food. Each cupboard was overflowing almost. I was undernourished, too thin. I looked forward to cooking extravagant foods and taking full care of myself.

It was at that moment that I began to cry. Not from sadness, nor pain. But from the sheer joy of my new situation and freedom.

I'm going to be okay now. He won't find me here. He'll never find me. Safe, I'm finally safe.

My tears turned to wild laughter.

Later that evening, I lay in the bath for almost two hours, until my skin turned as wrinkled as dried fruit.

I chose the room with the rocking chair and four-poster bed to sleep in. A deep weariness overcame me instantly. I couldn't remember the last time I was able to have a full night's sleep, nor could I recall the last time I'd felt true happiness. I sensed a deep understanding. I had already overcome everything terrible in life and now all I had to do was to heal. I climbed into the luxurious bed, not caring if the sheets were clean or not. Heavy with exhaustion, I closed my eyes.

I felt the house breathing softly, I felt the home watching over me and caring for me. I felt its kindness and compassion and the knowledge brought comfort. When I opened my eyes in the night and saw the rocking chair swaying gently, all by itself, I smiled and felt more at peace than ever.

In the morning, I wolfed down some toast and got to work. I found all the cleaning items a person could ever need to be crammed into a dark and small, almost hidden cupboard. I rolled up my sleeves and scrubbed, dusted, and hoovered. I washed everything and began to make sense of who had lived in the house.

I knew the owner had recently died, a gentleman named Albert, and I knew the home was now his daughter's possession.

I pieced together that the clothes in the main bedroom belonged to Albert and his deceased wife, Elisabeth. She owned beautiful clothing, cashmere, soft cotton, tailored linens, and fitted dresses.

I hadn't been able to bring many clothes, my suitcase contained just two old shirts and a single pair of jeans that were far too big.

I should wear her clothes, at least, just while I'm here.

So, I did. I washed them first and tumble dried whatever I could. I cleaned the bathroom and washed the wooden paneled walls along the hallway. Before I knew it, it was lunchtime and the doorbell rang.

I froze, terrified.

It's him! He found you! Hide quickly!

"Don't let him get me please," I begged the house. "Please."

My breath came in big ragged gasps as my hands shook. I dropped my bucket and threw myself in a corner and into a ball.

"No, no, no," I sobbed.

I felt the house wrap itself around me to protect me. It held me close until the feeling of peace returned and my panic subsided. The front door opened a crack as a grey-haired lady poked her head inside.

'That's the housekeeper,' the house whispered to me.

"Hello, is anyone here?" The lady called.

I stood, wiped my face, and smoothed down my clothes. The house filled me with the power and confidence I needed. I plastered a fake smile on my face and waved brightly as I walked toward her.

"Hi, I'm Anna," I told her. "I wasn't expecting anyone, I was cleaning."

"Hello! I'm Mary, I'm the housekeeper, well, I'm retired now. I wondered how you were getting on, that's all. I said to my husband, I better check on that young lady up at the house all on her own and see if she needs anything."

"That's kind. Thank you."

I was vaguely aware that I should offer her tea or coffee. But I felt as if she were trespassing on me and the house.

"Well, it's no trouble. How are you getting on, dear?"

"Just fine."

"Oh, I see. Well, I won't keep you then. If you need anything, I'm in the nearest house on the left."

"Thank you, I appreciate it," I said, because that's what people are supposed to say. I knew that.

Mary nodded and waved, she closed the door behind her with a sharp click.

I turned the key and drew the heavy bolts across. I didn't want her sneaking into the house again, into my house.

For the first few days, time passed quickly and smoothly. I took advantage of the soft breeze outside and hung baskets of washing out. The house looked immaculate, it was no longer neglected, it shone proudly.

At night I liked to lay in my kingly bed and smile. The house began to speak to me, not the odd sentences it whispered from day one, but long, intricate, and wonderful tales.

I learned that it was built in the nineteen hundreds, on old pagan land. The covered old well at the end of the massive garden was all that remained of the ancient, yet still powerful magic.

I learned that the house had many owners over the decades, although its favorite was Albert. He loved the home so much that he never left. The house had become his anchor and the chain to bind him was a short one. I envied him, even though he was dead, I felt a sting of sharpened jealousy that he was preferred.

The walls whispered a lullaby to me as I fell to sleep each night, a song half-remembered from my childhood.

One night, I woke to the sound of footsteps. A whole clammer of them outside, they clattered away on the wooden floor in the hallway.

I drifted across the room and peered around the door. I saw three children dressed in old-fashioned clothing racing about in a game of chase. One had blonde hair as yellow as summer wheat, the others had dark hair and curious clever eyes. I gently closed the door and left them alone. I understood the house was telling me its stories and showing me its precious happiest memories that were embedded within the walls.

"Thank you," I whispered and climbed back into bed. The sounds of the children laughing and playing lulled me back into a happy sleep.

When I awoke again, pressure pressed down on me and I hadn't been able to move, not one inch. I recognized the familiar feeling and I knew it would fade quickly. By the time I could move, I looked down at myself. My borrowed nightshirt was covered in blood.

"What have you done now?" He screamed. His voice sounded so close, but I knew it was impossible.

It's not real, he's not here. He's far away. He can't find you.

Reality blurred. Half of me knew I was stuck in a memory, one that was worn out and replaying again tiredly.

I screamed in confusion and the house came to my defense. Warmth engulfed me as I rocked back and forth.

"It's not real," I chanted. "It's not real. Not anymore."

The feeling of love spread its way all over me until my heart calmed its frantic beats. 'Safe,' the house told me. 'You're safe.'

I curled up into a ball and sobbed loudly. Like a mother's embrace, the walls and floor itself rushed to soothe me as the visions faded.

No blood see, there's no blood. Everything is okay.

It was hours before I could move properly again. My body felt on fire and my limbs hurt from tension. I soaked in the bath, unafraid to show the house the scars on my body while the house itself told me the tale of its birth.

An architect by the regal name of Alexander Booth-Chambers designed and built her from the ground up. He died in the house he had loved and refused to leave. The energy the house gave was the tie to bind, the unconditional love in bricks and mortar that most craved and still never found. I understood. I understood everything.

After my bath, the feeling of tranquility returned. I began to sort through Albert's belongings. I wrote neatly in my given notebooks and estimated prices. Was I right? I doubted myself entirely.

"Keep that," a deep voice from behind me spoke. I jerked and turned. Albert himself was sitting in one of the plush red armchairs I admired the most. He wore a smart shirt and cardigan, pressed trousers, and thick socks. He grinned and I liked his face straight away. He looked like a kind man, with one of those open, friendly faces of bright eyes and thick wrinkles that suited him. He was as refined as I expected.

"Hello," I said. I hadn't been surprised to see him, it somehow felt inevitable. I wasn't scared either, I felt sure the house had arranged for our meeting. If the home loved Albert, then I should, too.

"Keep that, I don't want that thrown away please."

I looked at my hands, I held a fat old compass peppered with rust.

"Shall I clean it?" I asked him.

Albert smiled and began to become translucent. As I watched, the deep red of the chair behind him started to show. He nodded and winked once, and in a single blink, he was gone.

The encounter hadn't troubled me, it gave me more of an incentive to have everything right and to work even harder. I cleaned that compass until its surface resembled a mirror. I placed it gently on the mantlepiece of the fireplace with great respect.

Later that same evening, the walls began to bleed. I watched, horrified, as blood poured down the freshly scrubbed stairs in waves. I saw it leak in massive streams down the main wall in the living room.

"What's happening?" I wailed. I felt afraid for the house and not for myself. I ran to the bleeding wall and pressed myself against it. I sang the same lullaby it had sung to me, I stroked the wet walls and told it I won't ever leave. I promised to stay, somehow. The bleeding stopped abruptly and I slid down the wall.

"I'm sorry you're in pain," I told the house. "I understand it. I really do."

The room shuddered and took a deep breath as I curled up aside it. I slept there all night, with one hand stroking the wall to comfort.

The next day, the house and I both felt wonderful.

'You have secrets,' it whispered to me.

"Yes, and someday I'll tell you. But not today."

Overnight, the blood had disappeared as if it were never there. I began to catalog Albert's treasures and I threw nothing away. He appeared once, he stood over me with a proud smile and dissipated in the way that fog is sometimes prone to do. Before lunch, I decided it might be best if I threw my suitcase down the old well. I don't know if I thought of doing that by myself, or if the house planted the idea inside me.

It was still by the front door, it stood abandoned near my coat. I grabbed it and padded across the dewy grass. The further away from the house I got, the colder I started to feel.

The emotions of terror and confusion began to overwhelm me. I fought off a nasty wave of dizziness that almost turned my vision black, I dropped my case near a dying bush and ran back inside. I shut the door firmly and slid the bolts across, my hands were shaking terribly. Being away from the house felt alien, all twisted and wrong. I knew then that I had to find a way to be able to stay. I knew that I couldn't leave, I wouldn't leave.

"I love you," I said out loud. I didn't feel shame or any embarrassment admitting that.

A wave of gratitude engulfed me in return for my confession. I placed my head against the walls and smiled.

I'm never leaving you, we belong together.

On the eighth day, I decided to have a rest day. I had been working hard every moment since I arrived. I cooked fresh soup from scratch in the clinical kitchen and I sat by the fireplace to eat.

A lady wandered through, just as I was lifting my spoon. She wore an elegant beige dress of lace and silk. She walked with an air of grace and I watched, astounded by her beauty. Her light-colored hair was tied up in a complicated knot and a string of pearls decorated her thin neck.

Her blue eyes, with wonderful long eyelashes, landed on me.

"Hello dear," she said in a magical, glorious voice.

"Hello," I answered.

"Have you seen Albert?"

"Not today, I'm afraid."

She smiled and revealed a perfect row of teeth. The sight of her made me breathless. She was so exquisite. She wandered straight through a wall and vanished. I laid down my tray and raced straight upstairs. I knew who she was, Albert's wife, Elisabeth. I yanked open the wardrobe in the room that was mine and rummaged inside. My hands landed on the texture of lace and I pulled the dress out, it was the same one the lovely woman had been wearing. It was slightly damaged and faded, but I shrugged out of my own borrowed clothes and slipped it on. Downstairs, among the boxes of jewelry, I found her pearls and I put those on too.

I danced in the living room to music only I could hear. The house laughed along with me. I felt deliriously happy. I moved in circles and raised my arms in the air. I cried happy tears and let them run down my face.

Then the doorbell chimed.

At first, I ignored the sound. I doubted the housekeeper would understand if she saw me and I assumed it was her. The knocking came moments later and I froze at the urgency hidden within the raps.

I crouched down low behind Albert's chair.

Nobody can get in, it's all bolted up. He can't find you.

The knocking sounded at the window and made me yelp in fear.

"Help me," I called to the house. "Please help me."

"Katherine!" a man's voice bellowed. "Open up, I'm here with the police."

Who's Katherine?

The voice sent a familiar chill of cold panic into my bloodstream.

The knocking started up again, even louder than before. I flinched and ducked down low.

"Open the door!" Another gruff and deeper voice ordered.

I clamped my hands over my ears, squeezed my eyes shut, and waited.

Please please please please, my mind prayed.

After two minutes of silence, I began to feel hopeful.

"Have they gone?" I asked. "They must have gone."

The house remained silent as I started to breathe easier. The tension in my body eased.

The sudden and massive sound of breaking glass made me scream in terror. Everything happened so quickly that it all became jumbled in my head. Glass broke on the rear door and bolts were undone. I screamed in fury as three tall men came in. Two policemen, both led by him. He'd found me.

In the distance, I heard the whiny voice of the housekeeper telling them to be careful as my eyes met his. He stared at me in horror.

"Go away," I seethed.

"Katherine, what have you done!" He breathed.

"I'm Anna, I'm Anna, I'm Anna," I shouted.

I curled myself into a ball and hissed like a cat. I couldn't begin to understand how he'd been able to find me. My heartbeat thundered in my ears as he walked softly towards me with his arms raised. One of the policemen moved to hold him back, but he shrugged them off and stepped forward as if he were approaching a wild animal. How I hated him at that moment. Anger filled me completely, all the way into the marrow of my bones.

"It's okay Katherine," he soothed. "We can sort this mess out."

"I'm Anna."

"No Katherine, you're not."

"NO. I'M ANNA!"

He shook his head and stared at me with pity. I hated that look as much as I despised him.

"Sir," one of the policemen said as his radio burst with static.

"It's all right," he told them. "Katherine is my patient. I'm a doctor, I can deal with this."

"The house will help me. The house loves me," I mumbled.

"Katherine, do you recall running from the hospital? Do you recall the events on the train?"

"I caught the train here," I told him.

"Yes, we know. The woman you met, the real Anna. She's awake now, she was able to tell us about the attack."

I closed my eyes and saw blood. Blood was all over my hands and lap, the dizziness made my head jolt. Someplace far off in my mind, I had the beginnings of an idea.

"No. I'm Anna," I wailed.

"You attacked the real Anna. You made friends with her and then attacked her. As soon as she woke up, she was able to tell us where you might be. You stole her job and her key. You are in a delusion. Trapped in one."

Is that true? It can't be. I'm Anna, aren't I? He's lying. He lies!

"I don't understand," I said because I didn't.

"I can sort this out. Come with us quietly, we can help you."

He lies. The house can help me, the house can protect me.

He turned to the waiting policemen.

"I have this under control. Give us a moment, please."

The bulky shapes of the police officers left the doorway. I saw my chance and I took it. I stood and darted past him as his eyes widened in alarm, I raced out of the door and up the stairs.

'Run,' the house told me, and so I did.

I sped down the hallway and ignored the shouts of shock and anger. I threw myself at the attic door, I fumbled for the handle and I yanked. The door opened without protest and I slammed it behind me. I drew the bolt across and stopped to wipe my tears away.

Memories collided as the present and past began to play simultaneously in my mind. I could smell the distinctive oily scent of the train station as I stood among the broken bits of furniture dotted around. I could almost hear the sounds of a train approaching and I could almost feel the vibration under my feet. I had caught a train, I had. That part was true.

I sat in one of the many spare seats with my stolen coat wrapped around me and I'd smiled at a pretty, smartly dressed young woman. She'd told me she was on her way to a new temporary job. One where she had to price up items in a rambling old manor house. A job just like mine.

I leaned heavily against an old oak cabinet and sank to the floor. I saw images play in my mind like an old movie, memories. White walls and nurses dressed in white, injections of clear fluid, and pink tablets. Him, sitting at his desk with his unread books displayed behind him, judging me, watching me.

A visit to an outside frightening world, an open gate, a chance to run, a chance to escape.

I am undone. I've come undone. I'm crazy, mad. Delusional, just like they said.

I saw blood on my hands and I wiped them on my pretty borrowed dress and when I looked again, the blood was gone.

"What do I do?" I asked the house, pleaded.

The walls and roof seemed to hold their breath while they reached a decision. In the corner of my eye, I saw Albert gazing out of a tiny porthole window.

"Albert," I said. "What do I do?"

He turned to stare at me, he held out a wrinkled hand towards me.

"Elisabeth," he smiled. "There you are."

"No, I'm Anna or Katherine, or…I don't know." I said.

Pounding on the attic door made me jump as I stifled a scream, I span around expecting to see a sudden rush of police officers about to snatch me. The door held firm and remained shut.

When I looked back, Albert had disappeared again. I felt the house give me a gentle nudge forward towards a window.

It was a large one I hadn't noticed before. It was big enough to fit a person through, big enough for me.

'You belong here,' the room told me.

And quite suddenly, I had the clarity to see what I had to do. Behind me, the door began to splinter and I glimpsed a single eye of his as he peered in.

"Katherine, please, you can get well. Please," he begged.

'He lies,' the house breathed.

I stepped forward and pushed the window open. I inched my way outside until I balanced on a ledge.

Two police cars sat like toy cars beneath me. A grey-haired lady stood between them wringing her hands in desperation, Mary, the housekeeper. All around me lay a patchwork of fields, all tinged with brown and orange colors. The sky had a glorious blue hue with an odd cloud dotted around. More clouds made their way toward me, come to witness my rebirth.

'Jump,' the house whispered to me.

My dress swayed in the breeze as the pearls around my neck turned cold.

I jumped.

* * *

Time moves differently here. Sometimes I see the children, sometimes I see Albert. I often see Elisabeth wandering by serenely. I even met the architect once.

New people live here now and the house doesn't like them, so I don't think they'll get to stay.

Flowers were left for me, a whole bunch just for me. He and the old housekeeper placed them gently on the drive, on the very spot I landed. The place where they covered my body with a sheet from the washing line. Roses, beautiful red roses. They faded quickly and started to rot. I never saw them again.

Time moves slowly or it moves too quickly, it depends on if I happen to be looking or not. I talk to the house a lot, and it talks back to me. I am wanted and needed. I am part of an exquisite wonder on an ancient land. Madness no longer plagues me. I am clarity.

I am alive in my death, this quiet melancholy existence of wandering fulfills me. Who would have believed that in death I would find my true life?

THE JUKEBOX

It began as an ordinary night in Mike's local. An ordinary pub, in the ordinary rural village he'd lived in his entire life.

Mike had been a regular for forty-nine of his seventy-two years. In his earlier years, he liked to visit twice a week to meet up with other landowners and farmers just like himself. They'd sit chatting over who had what new piece of farming equipment, who did what and why, and who might be deep in the red when it came to their crops and land.

For Mike, life is very different now. He visits every night, always from seven until nine, he sips his single pint of ale and sits by himself.

Sometimes, when Mike feels extravagant, he buys himself a pack of crisps or salted nuts. On rare occasions, the landlady saves him a slice of stale cake leftover from the lunch crowd.

Mike always sits in the far corner to watch people, it gives him the company he craves. Sometimes, he tries to fool himself and pretend he's part of their conversations.

But Mike likes to listen and, most of all, watch.

It's been three years since his wife Joy died, she suffered a massive cardiac arrest in the middle of her favorite soap opera while knitting herself a scarf, a scarf which remains unfinished, abandoned in her favorite chair.

Mike spends his days alone and his nights lonely. Once a week at six in the evening, his son calls on his old landline from London, the city he couldn't escape fast enough to. It's a pity phone call, one made purely from guilt and half-remembered promises.

Mike's son never comes back to visit the village he grew up in. He never brings his wife and new child, a grandchild Mike hasn't even met yet. Despite his endless plans to return soon. It's always soon.

Some families are held together by one member acting as the glue to bind. Joy was the glue for his family and since she'd gone, his relationship with his son has frayed, bit by bit, until the only thing remaining is the two-minute talk every Monday evening.

It's quiet in Mike's local, although it usually is on the weekdays. The same handful of lost souls gather in the one place they know they'll be accepted and left alone.

There are seven of them this evening. The usual weekday crowd, including Mike.

Max, the landlord, is a kind man, waiting eagerly for his retirement.

Jan, the landlady, Max's wife, and pub cook. She dreads retirement as much as she dreads her husband's presence.

Tom, a local teacher, brings his schoolwork to mark most nights with shaky hands. Mike thinks he has a drinking problem but really couldn't care less.

"Other folks are none of our business," his wife, Joy, used to say. Mike always keeps her words in mind, but he watches and he listens.

Sophie, or sometimes 'Soph', the pretty young barmaid. She's saving up to go off traveling. Mike listens to her planning her wild global adventures, adventures he wishes he had taken himself, with or without his wife.

Luke, Sophie's boyfriend. He has no idea his girlfriend's future plans don't include him.

Alan, the village shopkeeper. He's in permanent competition with the big new superstore and failing badly. Mike thinks he might give in soon and retire, another soul swept away in the recent developer's flood.

Mike knows everyone, he watches and he listens.

He rarely talks and he's often overlooked, but this is how he likes things to be.

He decides he'll go home at nine, a murder mystery might be on the box, maybe one he hasn't seen ten times already, and he knows he has a packet of his favorite chocolate biscuits left to enjoy, the good kind that won't go soggy as soon as they get dipped in tea. For Mike, small pleasures are all he has left.

Max and Jan huddle and whisper together behind the bar as Mike watches with interest. As Max leaves, Jan whispers to Sophie, she skips down the bar and whispers to Luke, who perks up and chases after Max.

Curious, Mike thinks, *a love triangle? It can't be!*

He resists the urge to laugh at his own idea.

He's seen plenty of affairs play out in the pub over the years, but he doubts this is one. Still, he feels interested.

The same nightly routine of small talk and pleasantries never usually changes. Except for that one night, when Alan had a heart attack, Mike stayed until past ten that night.

Everyone else had replayed the scene in hushed voices once Alan had been safely bundled inside an ambulance. They'd all been secretly thrilled that something had actually happened in the village, Mike had sat in his usual seat, overlooked, watching and listening.

"We have a surprise," Max announces loudly as Sophie squeals with delight. She clamps a hand across her mouth to silence herself.

All eyes look up, intrigued. A strange feeling begins to spread through Mike, excitement, or apprehension, he hasn't felt anything like that for some time.

"This," Max continues, "Is a jukebox, a good old-fashioned one, straight from an auction house."

Mike feels disappointed, he was hoping for fresh cake. He's not had a decent cake since Joy passed and besides, he doesn't much like music.

"You'll all have a token," Jan smiles, pleased, "one free go, one song, just for tonight because it's for weekends, I expect."

Mike grumbles under his breath and decides he won't be coming to the pub at weekends anymore.

Max and Luke drag in a large bubble-wrapped monstrosity, clattering and banging the door frame on its rusty trolley until it's been settled in the room.

A hush descends, and to Mike's surprise, it's teacher Tom that stands up to get close. He helps Luke rip into the wrappings and sets the Jukebox straight.

"It's so old!" gasps Sophie, "How old is it?"

"No idea," Max answers, "From the fifties I think, wasn't cheap either. It's been refurbished too, all updated. A pub burned down some time ago. This was salvaged from the fire."

He reaches around the back of the machine to uncoil the power wire.

Mike thinks of a huge fat snake he once saw at a traveling fairground years ago, a huge giant nasty-looking thing that had scared him so much it gave him nightmares for weeks, while Joy had stood transfixed at it in wonder and delight.

"Roll up, roll up, come and see the biggest beast from the Amazon," the snake handler had announced, "It has sharp teeth to bite!"

Mike shudders at the memory, he feels like this jukebox has teeth to bite too, lots and lots of sharp nasty teeth. He can't say why he feels this way, only that he does. It's the change, no doubt. Mike doesn't like change.

He likes his set routine, and now he feels his quiet reality shift beneath him. He doesn't want to sit in his usual chair and listen to music, loud songs he doesn't know and doesn't care to know. He likes peace, he likes quiet, he likes to watch, and he likes to listen.

"You're a grumpy old man," Joy once told him, and Mike supposes that he is.

Jan hands everyone a free token.

Hands greedily grab for them, everyone except Mike. He accepts his grudgingly and places it on the table where he can keep an eye on it.

There's nothing remarkable about the token. A simple piece of metal with '*ONE FREE PLAY*,' inscribed on both sides.

Yet, Mike watches his token warily, he feels that he should.

"These songs are old!" Sophie giggles.

"Almost as old as you!" She pokes Max in the ribs. He enjoys the attention but straightens up, looks at Jan, and plugs the machine straight into the mains.

Mike immediately feels the room turn colder, although no one else seems to notice the temperature drop.

He hears the pub door bolts slide firmly across, locking them all inside, but he doesn't move.

Mike watches and he listens. He doesn't move even as his spine and knees start to hurt badly, a problem that has plagued his later life and led to him using his trusty walking sticks.

He still doesn't move when he feels the pressure in the air change. His left ear pops, making him jump. He feels a tendril of fear creep slowly up his ravaged spine.

"It's alive," he whispers.

Don't be daft, you silly old man, his mind argues, but his instinct knows better.

The jukebox whirls to life, loud, bright, and vibrant. Its colored lights reflect pretty patterns on the ceiling and plain grimy walls.

For a moment, everyone stays silent, hypnotized by the light show.

Roll up, roll up, see its teeth.

"Load songs," Max squints and reads aloud, "It says to load songs."

He examines a modern screen, added Mike guesses, by the new refurbishment on the machine.

"Me first!" Sophie happily bounds over, she places her hands on either side of the machine as she bends forward, deciding. It's clear she doesn't recognize any of the music and she shrugs, looks briefly at the others, and shrugs again, grinning.

"I got one I think, I'm sure I know this song, it's by a blonde lady," she laughs and makes her choice.

Mike holds his breath, he doesn't know why he does this, only that he feels as if he should. Nothing happens.

"We all have to choose before it'll play," Jan says as she walks over.

It doesn't take her long to make her choice, the jukebox eats her token greedily.

Max is next, followed by Tom, then Luke, and Alan.

"Mike, c'mon, you're up," Jan reminds him.

She's always made an effort to involve him. He waves a hand in the group's direction, a signal for them to go ahead without him, he sips his pint as he watches and waits.

A hush descends, he hears his racing heartbeat thud in his ears.

Quite suddenly, the jukebox roars to life and begins to play Sophie's song, it starts with the chorus, the intro missing entirely.

It's broken!

"Waste of money," he mutters under his breath.

At first, Mike thinks Sophie has sneezed until he sees the mass of blood erupt volcano-like from her mouth. He watches as she clutches her chest, confusion all over her young face. She crumples quickly to her knees, hitting the floor and crashing down face first. A scream erupts from her mouth, turning the torrent of blood into bubbles as she thrashes around in panic.

It's Luke who reacts quickly while everyone else stares frozen and dumbfounded. Luke drops to his knees beside her and cries her name. Sophie screams once more, gurgling and whimpering in pain, she grabs him weakly and stills. Blood pools around her small body as her arm gives a single twitch.

Luke sits openly sobbing, Mike watches the room burst to life. Jan runs for the phone hanging on the wall behind the bar. Tom runs for the door only to find it locked. He pulls at the deadbolt again and again and it slides open, but still, the door remains shut tightly.

"Help," he pleads to the outside world, he bangs uselessly on the door. "Help us."

"It's dead," Jan shouts, sobbing and shaking the phone.

The jukebox stops abruptly. Mike watches and he listens.

Jan's chosen song begins to play.

Not one single person in the pub knows what to do when Jan starts to spin around in a wild circle, she spins and spins and spins.

Bottles from shelves she stands next to go flying to the floor, smashing and breaking in a rush of noise. The phone cord becomes wrapped around her throat as she flails on the spot, still spinning.

Max and Tom rush to her side, stepping over Luke who still cradles his girlfriend's dead body.

Jan is choking, her face turns purple as the phone is ripped from the wall in a shower of plaster and paint.

Neither Max nor Tom can catch a firm enough hold of her, the speed at which she spins is grossly inhuman. Max is shouting over the music, but Mike can't hear a word.

A screech of pure terror comes from someone's mouth and Jan falls dead to the ground, her spinning over. The jukebox falls silent.

"What the…!" Alan stares open-mouthed at the scene in shock, saliva drips down from his chin. Mike notices Alan starting to shake rapidly, he briefly wonders if he's going to have another heart attack as the front of his trousers turns wet from urine.

Mike watches and he listens, he has a small but impossible idea of what might be happening.

Max stands up from his wife's body, defeated and terrified. He turns to look at everyone, his pale face in shock with unnaturally wide eyes. All eyes look toward the jukebox as Max's own song begins to play, starting at the chorus.

By the time Mike looks back at Max, nothing but an empty space remains. He vanished within seconds, disappeared entirely.

Tom jolts like an electric shock passed through him, he bends forward and vomits.

Mike thinks he might pass out, but instead, he races to the Jukebox, slips on the floor, and tries to pull the plug. It won't move. He yanks desperately at the power cord, to no avail.

Roll up, roll up, come and see its sharp teeth.

Alan sits down heavily, struggling to breathe. He loosens his shirt and starts to hyperventilate and wheeze.

Tom's song begins to play. Surprisingly, Mike recognizes it. His son used to drive him and Joy mad with his music, playing it loudly and at all hours until Mike complained, only for it to be turned up even louder.

Tom stares frantically, pleading at Mike, then at Alan.

"Run man," Mike whispers.

Tom isn't moving, he's stuck in position as if he were a living statue. His eyes jerk around wildly and his mouth opens for one long, agonizing scream, which sounds more like a frenzied howl.

Those left in the pub hear a loud, resounding crack. Tom begins to fall to the floor as his upper body breaks clean away from his ankles as if his feet were nailed to the floor. Bloody splintered bone and feet are left behind, poking out of his shoes as Tom hits the ground. He shatters into pieces like glass, hundreds of cubes of jagged, red, meaty flesh tinged blue litter the floor.

Mike stares, trying to comprehend what he's seeing. His mind won't accept it, he feels his own sanity hanging by a thread and about to snap. He thinks he can spot one of Tom's eyeballs in the mess and the thought alone is enough to almost send his mind spiraling over the edge.

A loud banging sound snaps him back to reality. Luke is throwing himself shoulder-first at the main window. He picks up a stool and launches it, it bounces back so he pounds the glass with his bloody fist.

As Luke's song begins to play, he slides to the floor sobbing uselessly. He's on his knees crawling to Sophie's body when the fire starts.

First, there's a gentle poof of smoke, one so small that Mike thinks he's imagining it. A white-hot flame erupts from Luke's back, in seconds it turns into a furnace.

Luke throws himself down, wailing and screaming and trying to smother the flames out, they spread too quickly and eat him alive, engulfing him in less than half a minute.

The air turns rancid with the bitter smell of cooked flesh. What was Luke is now a charcoaled pile of ash.

Roll up, roll up. Plenty of sharp teeth to bite.

Alan is curled into a ball, muttering to himself. Mike thinks he might be praying, he always suspected he might be a religious man. Alan spasms once, little more than a bad hiccup, he turns sharply and vomits red and black liquid down his shirt and trousers. He jerks once more and lays still.

Mike watches and he listens.

Alan's song is one he doesn't recognize, but he hears the chorus well enough.

The pub is silent, all except for the whirling of the Jukebox, a humming sound Mike can feel all the way into his old bones, it lures him, calls him.

Roll up, roll up, Mike thinks, and so he does.

He takes a firm hold of his walking stick, collects his token, and finishes his pint in one mouthful. He walks unsteadily to the machine, careful not to slip on the blood and vomit-soaked floor, careful not to stand on the pieces that were once Tom.

His eyes don't work as well as they used to anymore, along with the rest of him. But Mike can just about make out the song list on the digital display box. He reads it carefully and thinks.

Heart of glass, he reads, so that's what happened to poor young Sophie.

Spin me around—a terrible and brutal end for Jan.

Road to hell—Max. Mike shuts his eyes in pity as he reads this one. He doesn't want to imagine the horror of his ending. Or would he instead be trapped there forever?

Cold as ice—Tom. Mike had suspected as much, it had looked to him as if Tom had been dipped in liquid nitrogen or some such thing. Frozen to death.

Light my fire—Luke. A horrific way to go, he thinks.

Poison—Alan.

It looks to Mike as if Alan had the easiest way out, the easiest death, or at least the most painless, although maybe he can be even luckier.

Mike feels exhausted by life and all the pain it brings for him. He wants his lonely days and lonelier, never-ending nights to come to an end.

He turns his token over in his calloused hands, thinking deeply. He knows a song, one his son used to play over and over, louder and louder, he knows it very well.

He puts his token in the hungry machine and makes his choice. He closes his eyes and waits, the beginnings of a smile form on his face.

Roll up, roll up.

Mike's old faithful walking sticks clatter to the ground, unwanted and abandoned.

The pub becomes empty of all life.

All that remains are the bodies of the unfortunate fallen.

Mike himself has vanished, just as the jukebox plays the chorus of Paradise city.

He always did like green grass and pretty girls.

AUTUMN OF '79

Our old neglected and worn-down house switched between sadness and happiness several times in the summer months of '79.

As the tensions inside increased, the land failed. Mold grew in high up hard to reach places, while our crops rotted away under the soil. The roof began to leak, windows cracked, and the health of our farm animals faded. We watched with a kind of helpless despair and waited for the inevitable collapse.

There were four of us children back then and it wouldn't have been an unusual sight to see us clustered together in one of our upstairs windows, watching the sky turn a blissful shade of pink as we each hoped the next day would be different.

We all enjoyed steaming up the windows with our breath to make stickman pictures with our fingertips while we giggled quietly.

In the cold months, the windows were permanently foggy, we took to leaving each other love hearts in secret.

We were close in our bond, but far apart in our personalities.

We were gifted with thick auburn hair and pale skin. Only Grace had been blessed with a sprinkle of freckles across her small nose and Edward had a sweet mole on his upper lip. I often pressed it and made a loud beep sound that always sent him off in fits of giggles.

During that fateful season of '79, I was newly fifteen and the eldest.

I was named Joanna, but almost everyone shortened it to Jo. I wasn't worth the extra two syllables, clearly.

I was a tomboy back then and I suppose I still am, I never quite grew out of my stubborn refusal to wear dresses or pretty things.

I worked hard on our seriously failing farm while I daydreamed of escaping to the city. The idea of working as a nurse or even as a secretary seemed the most glamorous of all possibilities, and one I deeply aspired to in private.

Justin had been fourteen that year, a true comic book geek even then. He possessed two of his very own science fiction comics and he read them to us all repeatedly.

He loved to draw us children and our parents, as comic characters or villains. He also loved to sleep, that boy could have slept away a whole week if I ever let him.

Every Sunday morning, we all have to get up real early and rush as quickly as we could through our chores.

After those were done, we had to attend church, only the threat of my father or a stick of dynamite could shift Justin from his bed in time.

Grace was eleven and my father's little princess, she was the only one of us able to calm his rages down and disarm him with a smile. Although, even she failed in those last few months.

Grace wore pretty but faded dresses and she adored the color pink. She was quick to laugh but prone to long sullen silences too.

I shared a room with her, the small one at the front of the house, it slowly became overcome by dolls and fluffy annoying teddy bears until nothing but an old broken bed of mine remained.

The bed was broken simply because the four of us spent our evenings huddled up on it until its legs buckled and gave in. We replaced the broken bits and propped it up with old books as best we could.

Finally, there was our beautiful little brother, Edward, aged eight.

Edward would now be diagnosed with Autism I'm sure. But in those days, none of us had ever heard the term and so he was sadly considered simple-minded. But only by the town folk who didn't know any better and never by us.

We all knew there was nothing simple about him at all. He was actually a very complex, clever, and extremely special little guy who was secretly my favorite.

I was drawn to him from the first moment I laid my eyes on him.

I usually took him along with me wherever I went, proud to show him off as if I were his mother myself.

Edward had the ability to sum up his needs, wants, and feelings with one word. He almost always chose that word as carefully as he could. He averaged just one word a day, although special exciting days like his birthday could have as many as three.

As the oldest, I had to get out of bed early every day to feed our cluster of chickens and collect the eggs. I would clean the coop and check the foxes hadn't attempted to get in as I went.

In summer it wasn't that hard, spring and autumn were fine too. It was the winter I grew to dread. The moment my feet hit those freezing draughty floorboards I was cold all over and stayed that way all day.

It never mattered how many layers I wore. In spring, the layers came off bit by bit like the shedding of skin. Outside, wildflowers would bloom everywhere you happened to look in thick, vibrant bursts of color.

It gave the area a joyful look it shouldn't really have possessed.

After the chickens, I would check the sheep and clean the barn, that was the job I hated the most on account of the smell.

Although those sheep were funny and entertaining, we had four of them and, of course, we named them after ourselves.

After that, it was back to the house to organize breakfast, usually eggs and coffee, cereals if we had any, or toast.

I'd take a tray to my parent's room and get Edward up and dressed.

More often than not, Grace got herself dressed, but I'd have to send her back whenever she tried to come downstairs wearing her own worn-out clothes back to front or even running around in Justin's clothes.

We were well known locally as the poor kids. We were never clean and none of us owned any clothes that actually fit. I felt guilty whenever I grew. Our clothes were old, passed down, or donated second-hand, to begin with.

My mother had been handy with a sewing needle, a skill she learned from her own mother. She handmade dresses for Grace or trousers for Justin and Edward as often as she could.

Mother loved to shop for new material, but that had been a rare event.

By early '79, she was under heavy pressure from our father to sell off some of our lands to the next family over.

The Richardsons. They were rich and owned shiny new incredible farming equipment. Their stuck-up daughter, who was my age, even had her own horse. Their whole existence seemed to me like something right out of the fancy magazines I sometimes found discarded in town and brought home for Grace.

Mr. Richardson visited a few days before everything happened. He made my parents an offer.

It was actually the day before his wife, Mrs. Elma Richardson, died of a sudden heart attack. Looking back, she was the first to die, I suppose.

She was found sitting in her favorite armchair in front of their big fireplace one morning, stone-cold dead.

Her death didn't stop Mr. Richardson from wanting our barren land.

The land that had been in my mother's family for generations.

"Are you selling a bit, Mother?" I asked her one afternoon as we hung out the washing.

"Looks like it," she snapped.

"Don't you want to?"

"You wouldn't understand Jo, It's what your father wants."

"But it's your land more than his, isn't it?" I asked.

"Hush now. Shut it."

She refused to talk about it, which is what my mother always did.

I was always being told back then that I wouldn't understand. They were wrong though, I understood everything just fine.

My father had been a kind man at some point, I assume. Until we hit hard times and his kindness was all eaten away by anger.

I think I know now that his failure to provide for his family took the greatest toll on him. But still, that's no excuse for his behavior.

He may have just been a bad man, I don't recall any occasions of real happiness with him. When he did spend time with us, which was rare. He was only ever half there and his hands would shake constantly.

When there was no money for food, there was always money for his whiskey.

One night, while my siblings were asleep in my bed. I heard my parents shouting at each other, or at least my father shouting at our mother.

"There were five pounds in that box, five whole pounds!" He raged.

I crept across the landing to sit on the stairs. The living room door had been opened slightly and I saw my mother sitting in an armchair with her head lowered. She sobbed gently into a handkerchief.

"We needed food," she whispered. "We have four mouths to feed."

"There needn't have been that many!" He spoke viciously. "There shouldn't have even been one."

I crawled away from my hiding place and crept back into my room. I don't think I slept that night. I lay awake trying to keep a foot or a hand on each of my sleeping siblings. I had a real longing to keep checking they were all still real.

I woke up very early the next day, just as it began to get light, and I walked downstairs as quietly as possible, avoiding every creaky step as I went.

My father had been asleep on the big armchair, the one my grandma Rose used to sit in to do her knitting, with a blanket half hanging off him.

I stood looking at him for a few moments. I couldn't bring myself to cover him properly or make him more comfortable.

Down by the side of him stood an almost finished bottle of whiskey. I tiptoed as silently as I could and picked it up by its neck.

My father grumbled and made a sound, rather than freeze, I made a dash to the kitchen and stood breathless to listen.

I dared to risk a look, but he still sat sleeping. I sniffed the bottle and jolted my head back. It smelt horrible.

I couldn't fathom why someone would drink something that made them so angry, so I tipped it in the sink and washed it away.

I needed to get my work done quickly. I wanted to take the children to pick fresh berries and blackberries. I was intent on teaching them which weeds we could eat too. Dandelions taste very nice if you find the freshest ones.

Our Grandmother Rose, who was originally Irish, had taught me which berries were good to pick and eat and which were poison to us. Our mother made a wonderful jam with the good ones and she kept promising to show me how it was done.

When the farm belonged to Grandma Rose, she ran it well alongside my grandfather.

We still had their old furniture, cozy old chairs, and knitted or crocheted throws. It wasn't until my own parents took over, after my grandparents' deaths, that everything good turned so bitter and driven to ruin, even the land itself was tarnished.

While the Richardsons' crops flourished, ours died or failed entirely.

After my chores were finished in the morning and after I checked that Justin had done his, the day was then our own. Although it was my responsibility to look after the children.

We rarely went to school, the way things were done was much different then. Rules and regulations came later, in '79 children could be and were overlooked. I and Justin were the ones to teach Grace how to read properly.

Edward picked most of it up too, but I believe he could have done that all by himself with his calm, quiet intelligence.

At the edge of our land, the land our father wanted to sell, sat a small pool I once thought of as a lake, but actually, it was just a large pond.

It had a big, ancient, solitary tree overlooking the edge. Years before, Father had made us a tire swing from the remains of an old tractor wheel, made sturdy with thick solid rope and clever knots, hanging from the biggest branch. We all loved to play there together.

We liked to swing on the tire and drop into the cool pool if it was summer. In autumn, we collected every crispy leaf we could find and piled them up to land on instead. We all loved that wonderful crunching sound the leaves made.

It was there, at our favorite place, on a bright chilly afternoon, when we first met the swapping lady.

If I remember correctly, it was Justin who named her the swapping lady, but that came long after. She had many names by the end, but at first, she was simply the lady.

It was an ordinary day, that particular morning had already been difficult for me.

The chickens had laid no eggs for breakfast, the sheep were sickly and we couldn't afford to help them.

I overheard Father telling Mother days before that we were already in the red with our local vet. They wouldn't come out until it was paid in full.

I hadn't understood what that meant then, being in the red. Only that it was something very bad.

Justin hadn't wanted to get up and do his chores, so I did his, too. My father had been angrily hungover, Grace had been upset because her favorite patched-up dress couldn't be fixed again. My mother had sat alone in her bedroom crying softly.

Only Edward had been trouble-free that day.

My perfect little brother. I led him and my siblings away from the house. I packed us a little picnic from the scraps I found in the cupboards, stale old biscuits, and forgotten jams, even an old flask full of milk.

I was hoping I could fill the basket with fresh berries on a walk down the Lane.

I remember I was hungry, I often went without food in those days, so my siblings had more to eat. I never minded, my life had seemed a little brighter when they were happy.

In the distance, we silently watched our parents get into our old car and leave for our neighbor, Mrs. Richardson's funeral, dirt kicking up behind them as they left.

I was laying down, stretched out on a worn old sheet by the water, promising myself that I wouldn't grow up to be like my parents or ever take to drinking whiskey.

I was trying to record the feeling of the sun on my skin, in the childish hope that I might be able to conjure the sensation in wintertime.

I watched the clouds, eager to find shapes, and at the time, I believed that those same clouds would come around again the year after.

Grace sat next to me, making daisy chains for us all to wear with calm patience and determination. She was humming a pretty tune, a song from church.

Memories can be fickle sometimes, and that particular piece of the puzzle has sadly slipped away, although it seemed important at the time.

"Jo," Justin whispered quietly.

He stopped pushing Edward on our tire and stood still.

I sat bolt upright. I recognized the nervousness in his voice and followed his gaze.

An extraordinarily beautiful lady had joined us quite silently. I watched as she stepped out from behind the trees. All of us were surprised by her sudden appearance and all we did was stare blankly at her.

It's different now, but in those days, strangers in our town were rare, almost unheard of. Strangers that looked like her seemed an impossibility.

My mind pieced together wrongly that she must be a visitor from the Richardson family out exploring the countryside instead of attending the funeral.

I felt my face turn red as I stood up to take charge.

"Can I help you?" I said.

The stranger wore a beautiful beaded white dress with colored embroidery along its hem, her feet were bare and decorated with a pretty tiny bell chain around one ankle that jingled whenever she moved.

Long black hair, all the way to her waist, fell smooth like liquid. She had the most beautiful angelic face I had ever seen, and even now I've never seen another face quite like hers.

So many thoughts spun in my mind, but mostly, I wanted to be her or to be near her.

I took a few steps her way as if she were a magnet pulling me.

"Grace, don't stare," I hissed, even though I was doing the exact same thing.

Our beautiful stranger smiled at us all, one by one. Her gaze shifted, starting with me, then Grace, then to Justin, and finally settling on Edward, who swung lazily back and forth on the swing.

"May I help you?" I said again, louder this time and with as much authority as I could find.

"Maybe," came her reply, and she smiled serenely.

Her voice sounded almost musical, but had a smoothness to it, a kindness to it that calmed us all. She seemed so different and other-worldly.

I had no idea what to make of her, or what I should even do.

"Are you lost? Are you here for the funeral?" I asked.

In my mind, I imagined her to be a queen from the land of the Fae folk grandmother Rose talked about or even a princess.

"Everyone is lost", she smiled. She walked over to our swing very gracefully, almost regally.

"I don't like funerals. But I was here for the death," she said and laughed a little.

I started to feel nervous and it struck me as odd that an adult would say something like that. She had a way about her that set my nerves jangling and everything felt strange for a few seconds, but exciting too. I had a wave of dizziness, so I sat back down on the sheet with my tummy rumbling.

I wasn't sure why the lady was talking in riddles and why she was even talking to us in the first place, usually no one bothered. Adults puzzled me in those days.

Most of them still do, actually.

She stopped in front of the tire and gave it a little push.

Edward could be notoriously difficult when he wanted to be. He disliked new people and he often screamed if any of the town folk came too close to him on our rare trips out.

He always needed one of us to hold his hand and I never minded taking the roll.

I braced myself for a scream that never came.

Instead, my little brother climbed off the tire and took her hand. I felt a sudden pang of jealousy mixed in with surprise.

"This one isn't so lost", she said and the two stared at each other, smiling contentedly.

On her hands and knees, Grace crawled over and sat at her feet, she received a gentle pat on the head for her trouble.

Absurdly, the scene in front of me reminded me of the pretty colored glass picture windows in our church, one of the biblical scenes they told us had really happened.

It wasn't often that I was ever stunned into silence, but so far, she had me stumped.

Confused and unable to think of a single thing to say, I sat and looked at her.

"Are you new?" Justin asked, and broke the silence.

"No, not at all," she smiled.

I and Justin stared at each other, both waiting for the other to do something.

The lady walked serenely over to me with Edward and sat down on our old sheet as Grace skipped after her. She had a captivating scent of wildflowers and sharp smoke.

Grace gently placed a daisy chain on the stranger's head like a crown.

"How wonderful!" She beamed as Grace clapped with delight.

I began to have a really bad feeling. I thought of our old dog Alfred when he would sense a fox or badger that none of us could see and his hackles would raise. But as soon as the lady looked at me, I felt fine and suddenly everything seemed quite natural and normal again.

I thought of our church's lessons of Christian values, the rules to share and help strangers because God had wanted things to be that way.

"Are you hungry?" I asked her.

"Yes. Quite often."

A short, clipped laugh escaped me, and I clamped a hand over my mouth in shame. I didn't know why her reply was so funny, but I felt desperate to laugh. As soon as the bubble of laughter formed, it was gone again.

I looked at the lady, her eyes were the darkest of brown. They were almost black and her skin glowed perfectly, like one of the dolls Grace sometimes carried around.

"We don't have much," I told her. "But enough to share with you."

I lifted the cover off the basket we had so we could eat.

I knew there wasn't enough, not for the four of us and certainly not for five, and so I lifted the cover slowly in embarrassment.

I found fruit piled high on top of the dry biscuits, jam, and bread I'd salvaged from the cupboards.

Tucked in between the fruit were chocolate bars and in those days, we only ever had chocolate at Christmas, big bars that were given to us by our church as gifts. The year before, our father had eaten every bar all by himself until he was sick.

"What!" I gasped. "How?"

I think I believed then that our mother arranged the surprise. That was the only explanation I had, or at least, that's what I tell myself now.

I must have known, even in a small part of myself, that it was impossible. But I pushed the thought away as far as I could get it and told myself a beautiful lie.

In reality, we had no money for treats, and the only fruit any of us ever had hung from the tree at the back of our land, all sour and hard.

"A feast!" The lady sang in delight and clapped her delicate, pretty hands. "How kind you are!"

Only Justin narrowed his eyes, suspicious. But like me, he chose to ignore his instinct and shrugged.

Grace dived in first as I tried to divide everything equally, always the peacekeeper.

The food from our own bare cupboard lay neglected and abandoned at the bottom of our basket.

I admit, the taste of those big red apples and juicy peaches, the sweetness of the chocolate was the best I ever tasted in my whole life. I saved the pomegranates and pumpkin for later. I had an idea to try and make a pie or soup.

We were delighted, happy in a way I still struggle to describe.

All four of us children had grown so used to being poor that we knew we had to treasure simple pleasures and grab the good bits of life as hard as we possibly could and try to never let go.

I caught the woman's eye and she winked at me, something passed between us then, a kind of electricity and I had such love for her at that moment. I wasn't at all sure if I should or if it was wrong.

I wanted to stay with her. I was in complete awe.

Abruptly, she stood up and smoothed down her pretty dress.

"Back tomorrow!" She smiled and walked away, back towards the rich house. I hadn't known if she meant it as a statement or invitation.

"Don't go," Grace whined, and our lady paused. She stared at us all in turn and waved.

She didn't disappear as such, it's just that one minute she was there, walking away with her dress billowing behind her, and when I looked again, she was gone.

"Who was she?" Justin gasped, amazed, with his cheeks full of color. "Where did she even come from?"

I shrugged. Everything had turned cold. I felt as if I'd experienced something truly remarkable by just being in her presence and then lost it again, the shock of the fall back to our reality was hard to handle.

A sadness overcame me. All that joy snatched away and now all we had to look forward to was our parents arguing and difficult, never-ending chores. I wanted to run after her, I jerked a little as I almost stood to chase her.

"Happy," Edward announced and snapped me out of my thoughts.

"Me too," Grace mumbled with a mouthful of apple.

"We'll wait here all day tomorrow," Justin said, and not one of us disagreed.

I felt glad it wasn't going to be a church day, I could rush the chores and have everything done early.

"We will," I told them. "I bet she's an aunt or something or a cousin to the Richardsons and I bet she's a film star or a ballet dancer too."

We all settled on that explanation and stayed at our pond for another couple of hours.

I went back to laying down, gazing at the clouds and trying to make shapes out of them. I failed over and over, my mind had been too full of her.

We saw our parents' car kick up dirt, signaling their arrival home as we looked at each other.

We never knew back then if we were to go home or stay where we were.

We had a code we all knew to follow carefully.

If our mother waved, it meant Father wasn't drunk or angry and it was fine to go home.

If she didn't wave, that meant we should stay out until almost dark and that there wouldn't be any supper.

She didn't wave that day, but for once, it hadn't mattered.

Later that night, I lay in my bed wide awake, staring at the cracks in the ceiling. Whenever it rained, the roof leaked. I often wondered if the whole lot would come crashing down on my head someday.

I only hoped that it didn't happen on one of the nights we all slept directly under the worse bit.

Grace was breathing softly from across the room.

I'd taken a book from my mother's shelf, one my grandmother had given to her when she was a girl, a book all about fairy tales. I wasn't allowed to do that, take books. But I was looking for our lady in its pages.

Our door crept open and I shut my eyes tight and faked being asleep. Justin sneaked in, quickly and silently trailed by Edward.

Our parents were shouting downstairs, a vicious argument. But I knew better than to try and intervene again.

My father had hit me the last time I tried to stop them, my ears had rung for weeks after.

They were shouting about land again and it sounded as if my mother was still refusing to sell any. I heard the word divorce and then the shouting had really begun, I hadn't known what that word meant then, but it sounded to me like another scary, bad word.

"I can't sleep," Justin said and climbed onto my bed, curling up at the end just like our old tabby cat used to. Edward clambered in beside me, he often did and I never minded, in winter with no heat, he became my human hot water bottle.

"Neither can I," I admitted.

Grace moved then, she sat up and wrapped a blanket around her little shoulders. She made her way to us and I reached out to hug her.

What a sight we must have been, four dirty kids in rag pajamas, hungry and piled up in an old bed.

"Who was she, Jo?" Justin asked. "I mean, who was she really?"

I shrugged because I truly hadn't known.

"Maybe she was just a very pretty lady, but ordinary," I suggested. "I looked for her in the fairy book, but she isn't in it."

"No," Edward mumbled.

"Maybe she's a famous actress in a London theater," I said.

"But…everything felt…I don't know, a bit like a dream," Justin shrugged. I nodded in understanding, glad he felt that way too.

"She looked like an angel, so maybe she was one," Grace spoke shyly. "I've been praying for one to help us."

"Me too," Justin whispered.

"No," Edward stated. We all stared at him.

"Who is she then?" Justin asked.

I held my breath and waited to see if Edward would say one more word. I longed for him to say something remarkable. Instead, he held up his arms and spread his hands as far as he could reach.

"What does that mean?" Grace whispered, and Edward only shrugged.

"Well, I think she's an angel. They help sad children. Church said so," Grace announced.

Tears ran down my face. I tried so hard to protect them and I was failing.

How innocent we were. Sometimes our naivety makes me smile.

For us, the lines of life hadn't become blurred yet. None of us were tainted by the outside world or even knew much about it.

We were all raised on Christian church teachings, the endless battle between good versus evil.

Of Eden and Adam and Eve, the flood, and Noah's ark. We knew of a vengeful God that played mean tricks on his own children or drowned them if they disobeyed.

The only book we were officially allowed to read was the Bible, and we each had our favorite stories.

By age fifteen, I thought the Bible was the same as the fairy tales of my grandmother's fairy folklore, metaphors, and fables. I still pretended to believe in church teachings, just to keep the peace.

In my own mind, people were either saints or sinners. The righteous or the damned. But magic still existed too, in our young imaginations. I don't think you lose that belief until you grow older.

Adults forget the things children once knew to be true.

"Maybe she is an angel then. She must be?" Justin sighed happily.

We all ended up settling on that explanation, one that gave us hope and made us believe that God had really heard our pleas and seen our sadness for himself.

"Let's keep watch, in case she comes back early," Grace said.

So we did.

We spent the rest of the night taking turns to either sleep or watch for our angel lady.

In the middle of the night, it had been my turn. I liked to look at the stars if they were out and I tried to imagine what made them shine the way they do.

I listened and heard the front door swing open with a clatter.

I watched our father stumble out of the house and zig-zagged his way to our tire swing. He often did that, so the sight was quite normal.

I hated the fact that he used our swing, it made me feel as if he was tarnishing our special place by just being there.

I think I fell asleep, I must have. The last thing on my mind had been her. I pictured her face and the way she'd radiated that warm kindness. I prayed she'd keep her word and come back. Our angel.

It never once crossed my mind that she was something else entirely.

I woke up early, too early even for me. I struggled to open my eyes and straight away, I wondered what had woken me.

Mother's screams tore through the early morning mist. I bolted from my crooked bed and ran downstairs.

I knew her screams came from outside, I assumed our sheep were extremely ill or that she'd been hurt by my father. Neither option beat the other one.

At church, a couple of weeks before, Mother had told everyone that she'd banged her face on a cupboard at home. She always used that same excuse to explain away the bruises whenever she was asked.

I don't think anyone ever believed her story, but no one had come by or done anything to help either, they never did.

I raced down the stairs holding the banister tightly and ran out of the open door.

"MOTHER?" I shouted.

I heard a whine coming from my left and so I headed that way, the sun had almost come up so it wasn't too difficult to see.

Because of the mist, it was almost a black and white scene facing me, my mother stood frozen at the edge of our pond, her hands wrapped in her hair and pulling it out in clumps. I just made it in time to stop her from falling to her knees.

In the pond, face down, was my father. An empty whiskey bottle half floated beside him.

Straight away, I assumed he was dead.

I dropped down beside her and waited for her to catch her breath.

"Go and fetch the police, Mother," I told her. "Pull yourself together and fetch them."

She looked at me with a vacant, glassy expression, and I shook her shoulders firmly. "GO", I repeated. "Quickly now."

And she did, she snapped out of her shock and wobbled across our lawn.

I stood and looked at my father, wondering if I should pull him out and attempt mouth to mouth, just like they showed us once at school.

In my mind, I pictured my attempt working, and of him coming to life again. Coming back to upset us, to shout at us, and hurt my mother. If he lived, he'd spend every penny on whiskey again.

I closed my eyes and asked God what I should do. I looked at the night sky and felt a gentle breeze on my skin. I felt certain God would want me to save my father, or at least try. But I didn't, I stayed where I was and I left him floating.

I think I knew I was doing something bad by not doing anything at all, I felt it deep inside.

I sat down on the damp grass and I stayed sitting and watching, even when a line of bubbles left his mouth and popped up to the calm surface.

At the border of our property, tall rows of trees lined up like soldiers, the bushes between them parted and our angel lady stood half-hidden among them.

I should have felt surprised to see her, but I didn't.

We stared at each other silently. She nodded at me once, then slowly melted backward at the sound of our car coming and being followed by a siren.

I think I understood then that somehow, she'd been responsible and I loved her for it.

The start of the next day is a little jumbled up in my mind.

I think our brains can record specific memories and play them back to us when we need them or sometimes when we least do.

Some of my recordings are locked away tightly in my mind. I have to blow off the metaphorical dust to get them to play again.

I do recall that our home bustled with activity. Our local policeman came with a serious-looking spectacled man. He drove a grey van and carried a long bag for the body.

An endless stream of town folk and neighbors, all bringing dishes of food and kind words called by. Really, I suppose they were eager to hear all about what had happened to my father.

The phrase 'too much whiskey' became overused within hours, always followed by loud tuts and with a sad shake of the head.

The police questioned me and my mother, of course, but it was all half-hearted. It was clear enough to everyone what had happened. I mentioned nothing of our angel, not a single word. I even tried not to think of her, in case they could tell.

Mother was the one to tell my siblings that our father had drowned, all because of the whiskey. There were even fewer tears than I expected and no tantrums at all.

I still had to clean the barn and let the sheep out to graze and I was on my way back

To the house when I heard my mother softly singing for the first time in my short life.

She was sorting through all the gifts we'd been brought, all the tins and packets had been put away and the cupboards overflowed. There was even an envelope full of money sent to us from the Richardsons.

"Jo," she smiled. "My Joanna, your father had a life insurance policy. We're going to be rich now."

She laughed so hard she had to sit down at our table.

"We can buy new things, make a list, all three of you, and we'll keep the house and the land. Things will change now, it'll all change."

"Three of us?" I asked her, "You mean four of us, mother."

"Ah yes, of course," she sang.

I hadn't understood her, but I expect she'd felt relief, mixed in with sadness and maybe a new sense of freedom too. She hadn't celebrated my father's death, none of us had. We'd all been a little sad in our own way. But he had truly been a bad man, I only wondered if he'd gone to heaven or not, I thought not.

Mother gave me a few packets of crisps, another rare treat, and I went to join my brothers and sister. I dished the treats out and sat down with them, I only felt numb and more than a little confused.

"Are you all okay?" I asked my family.

Grace grinned, crisps spilling from her mouth. Justin gazed off in the distance. Little Edward was pulling bits of grass up then blowing the strands away. I knew he was feeling overwhelmed by the busy morning we'd all had and needed some time in the quiet to process it all.

"Did he suffer?" Justin asked abruptly.

I closed my eyes and thought very carefully about how to answer.

"I don't know. He passed away before we got to him," I answered. I wasn't really sure if that was the truth or not, but I suppose I knew it might be a lie deep down.

"Will he go to heaven?" Grace asked.

I shrugged, that question was on everyone's mind it seemed and I had no idea if he would or not.

"Mother says everything will change now, and I believe her. We all have to make a list."

"What of?" Grace said.

"I'm not really sure," I continued. "Things we need, I think."

"Comics then," Justin smiled, and we all lightened up.

"Dresses for me, pink ones, and new dolls!"

For me, the world shifted a little and righted itself. The boulder that had sat on my chest for as long as I could remember lifted a little. I started to think that maybe I wouldn't have to leave at sixteen after all. I could stay with my family, help on the farm more, and even start to enjoy my life.

A bubble of joy rose up and a broad smile lit up my face.

At that moment, a world of possibilities opened up and it felt like the worst things we would ever face in life had already happened to us and we survived.

"Life can only get better," I said, not at all realizing how wrong I truly had it.

"Happy little children," came our angel's velvety voice.

She stepped out from behind the trees and I wondered how long she'd been there, listening to us. My skin felt hot the moment I saw her. The scent of lavender trailed after her. A fizzing sensation started up in my head, and my mouth felt like sandpaper.

Edward stopped pulling at the grass and made his way to her without hesitation.

Justin's cheeks turned red, and Grace squealed excitedly.

I wanted to say so much to her, but as soon as I saw her, every single one of my planned words left my mind.

"Our father died," Grace blurted out. "Cause of the whiskey drink."

"Oh dear," the woman said without any emotion at all, she raised an eyebrow at me.

"Are you an Angel?" Justin suddenly asked her.

Our lady wore a different dress that day, one that had long sleeves and spilled all the way to the ground. It was blood red with swirling patterns on the hem and decorated with curious half-moons. She looked even more perfect than before. My heart skipped several beats while my ears thudded.

"Is that what you think I am?" she asked Justin.

He nodded and smiled very shyly as his cheeks burned red.

I could smell the slight smoke and wildflowers again. She had such a presence about her that I couldn't help but stare. Being around her made you feel good all the way inside, right into the marrow of your bones.

"We learned about angels in our church," Grace stated matter-of-factly.

"Church," our lady said, and waved her hand dismissively. "This should be your church."

She spread her pretty hands out and pointed to the woodlands.

I saw that her hair had pretty flowers threaded through and her nails were painted red to match her dress. None of us answered her. I presume that we hadn't understood what she meant.

I do now, of course, I both understand and agree.

"What's your name?" I asked as I watched Edward hug her leg. She leaned down to hug him back and gently stroked his hair.

"I forgot to ask before, sorry. I'm Joanna or Jo, this is Grace, Justin," I said as I pointed to each of us in turn. "And you have hold of Edward."

"I have many names, Joanna or Jo, it all depends on who it is that's doing the looking."

"I don't understand...." I frowned, lost. My words trailed away as she smiled and sharply turned her head to look straight at me.

Those moments are hard to describe and I doubt I can ever do them justice, even now, after thinking about it every day for all these years.

The second her eyes met mine, my family froze in position. I had the gut-wrenching sensation of falling endlessly down and down, although I never physically moved. Or at least, my body never moved. My mind was taken elsewhere.

Her beautiful face melted away as her mouth stretched impossibly wide, becoming a black abyss filled with tiny pinpricks of light and what I think were stars and universes existing inside.

I had no choice but to watch her eyes flash from black to blue to brown then, green.

My mind fought to hold on to my own sanity as I was hit with a sudden rush of images and powerful emotions, a movie happening only in my head and only for me to see.

I saw three bare-chested Native American Indian men with bright, painted markings decorating their skin. They rode on horseback and raced across the plains. One fell down, injured by enemy bullets. Two of the remaining men were standing over the enemy soldiers who lay down weapons in frightened surrender.

I watched as a pretty woman in a run-down wooden shack held a newborn baby to her bare breast happily, while a man I felt was her husband lay suddenly dead on the floor.

I witnessed an old-fashioned wagon half hanging from a steep cliff. Children were saved from the fall while their savior fell to his death, his broken body hit rock after rock as he bounced the whole way down.

I saw a tall gaunt man facing death and rotting from the inside, a terrible blackness was overtaking him, then the same man was healthy as his beautiful wife suffered his fate instead.

Tears began to fall down my face.

The pain and decisions each person felt hit me, wave after crashing wave.

I saw the father of the Richardson family handing over a newborn baby to our angel lady and then becoming rich. I felt Mrs. Richardson's pain as she swapped her life for the chance to hold that traded baby once more.

Our lady, our angel woman, was a being who could become so many things. She made trades, swaps, and took the energy of a whole person for herself. The last image filled me with complete terror and I screamed inside my mind.

One final image was shown to me, one of my very own mother standing at our pond, in the near dark, illuminated by moonlight like a spotlight. Bruises covered her haggard face as she knelt to make a pact with our lady. A pact to end my father's life and bring the family wealth, in exchange for Edward.

The lady wasn't there for us, she hadn't come to help us and be part of our story. She was conjured or summoned to deal and trade with our mother.

"No," I pleaded out loud as the visions came to an end. "Please, please no."

The despair and betrayal tore at my heart. Panic overspilled.

"You're a demon, a devil," I spat.

She walked towards me and crouched down to look me in the eye.

Her face returned to its perfect beauty.

"I owe you no explanations," she told me. She stroked my face and wiped my tears away. She reached out to touch my shoulder.

I think she did it because I loved her, and she knew it. God help me I couldn't help but love her.

There were no images as her hand landed on my skin.

She gave me the knowledge I believe.

I knew in a single moment that our angel was something far older and much more ancient than anything dreamed up by any religion on Earth.

She wasn't evil or good. But something other, a force beyond mine or anyone else's understanding.

She was legend and folklore, the origin of all myths. She had many faces and hundreds of masks.

She took human form for her exchanges, for her deals and swaps. A form stolen from our own minds, ideas, and concepts taken from our world and cultures. She adapted as we did. Changed as we did. Grew as we grew.

She had many names. Many stories. She was a living collection of everyone she took, but an endless empty void, too.

Eternal, infinite, and timeless. She was something I couldn't and still can't comprehend. She was hate and love, pity, and pain. Always in motion, but then still, listening and watching. Waiting.

I knew that she had already taken my brother, my Edward. I knew he would now cease to exist but also exist forever simultaneously. My brother, becoming everything and nothing. For us, he would be gone. I was powerless.

I understood that minds and memories would be altered and taken away, Edward would be scrubbed from existence. Anyone who knew him would forget they ever met him. That's how she had remained so hidden.

I understood that she would let me keep my memories of my little brother. If I ever told anyone the truth or ever spoke of her, she would come for me and I would receive no mercy.

＊ ＊ ＊

In the days after, Mother, Grace, and Justin's lives slowly settled and improved.

As soon as the swapping lady left, Edward was erased from the minds of those who loved him and of those who knew him. Except for me. He stayed firmly in my mind and always in my heart.

I cried night after night, I missed him dearly. I felt the hollow loss every moment of the day. At night when I slept, I dreamed of her.

I carried on with my chores, I cooked and I cleaned. I existed, but I failed to live.

In the months that followed, I stayed at the farm. I looked after our animals and our land. I kept going for Grace and Justin.

My mother died three years after my father, at midday exactly. From a sudden cardiac arrest while we were both in the barn, milking the cows.

At least, that was the official report.

Just before midday, I left the barn and waited outside for a short time.

When I returned to the barn, I made no attempt at CPR.

I did not call an ambulance until twenty minutes had passed. By the time help arrived, it was, of course, too late.

In those three years, I had grown to hate my mother deeply. The woman who chose wealth and comfort over her own precious, beautiful child.

My mother had lived happily for three years with wealth from the life insurance policy.

I at least allowed her that.

On the night before Mother died, I told my brother and sister what had really happened with the swapping lady. They listened carefully to my hushed voice and they believed me, even going as far as recalling the odd, slight memory of our lost brother.

Once I spoke of him out loud, the spell became broken, as promised.

While we were sitting on my bed in mine and Grace's bedroom, like we used to, I told them my plan. They agreed.

I walked slowly to the pool and waited. I knew she'd come. She knew I'd spoken about Edward and spoken about her. I felt her listen, I felt her presence with us, with me.

It didn't take her long to arrive. This time, she was wearing a stunning gown of shimmering gold and blue. I won't lie and pretend I didn't enjoy seeing her, my heart became overjoyed at the sight of her.

"I want to make a swap," I told her.

"Of course you do, Joanna or Jo," she answered. Her voice was as beautiful and musical as ever.

"My mother and I, but only when my natural death is about to occur, in exchange for Edward back."

She threw her stunning head back and laughed.

"The sacrifice of your mother is sufficient for the boy," she smiled.

"No, me too. Upon my natural death. Please."

The swapping lady drew back sharply and circled me once like an angry cat. I felt a kind of sharp clarity, a longing.

A grin played on her beautiful mouth as she held her delicate hand out.

"Deal," she said. "Midday for your mother."

I cried as we made our pact. My tears were not from sadness.

We had Edward back the next day. He was returned a few hours after our swapping lady had been to collect our mother. Our memories were returned along with him and we became a real family again.

I and Edward remained at the farm. Grace married, but stayed close. Justin also married, eventually, and chose to live at the farm, too. His new wife joined our family. We grew and we thrived together.

Love replaced the hate in the ground. Our bonds healed wounds.

* * *

Sixty years have passed since I last saw our lady. Sixty years since our pact. I often wander to our pool, where our tire still swings, in the hopes of seeing her again, but I never have. Yet.

I know that someday I'll see her again.

I'm old and I'm tired.

I'm ready to leave this earth and she knows it. I expect she'll be back soon. Very soon. Especially now that I've spoken about her again.

I won't pretend I'm not looking forward to it.

MURDER MOST HORRID

I'd like to tell you a story and I need you to understand that it won't be a romantic, pleasant account. After all, this story is a twisted tale of love and pain. Those two infinite and exquisite emotions that go hand in hand as if they belong together when they shouldn't.

Love is red, or so they say.

Pain is more of an endless, consuming darkness, at least, it is to my mind. Everything in my head is black now. So black that it's as if I went in with a brush and painted it to look that way.

Love hurts, they say that too.

Although hurt gives the impression of a wound that can heal, a sensation that will most certainly fade in time and leave nothing behind but a flimsy scar. One you might glance at from time to time until you forget how you even came to have it in the first place.

True pain, the deepest of all, doesn't scar. It leaves behind a gaping wound. One that oozes misery until the infection deep within spreads and kills you dead.

True pain doesn't submit, it festers and it rots. It turns a shiny bright soul into a woman like me, one draped in a mold and with a single-minded focus and determination.

One so enraged by bitterness and betrayal that a sharp knife in a hand becomes the one talisman to end all suffering.

They also say that the ending of all stories must have redemption or a happy ending at the very least. Perhaps one of clear skies and autumn sunsets. Lovers strolling hand in hand, a united pair lost in their own secret world created between them.

Mine ends in fire and blood. Lots and lots of blood.

I'm a kind and quiet girl. Everyone says so, so it must be true.

I cross my legs and wrap my arms firmly around myself, tightly, as if I need my limbs to bind and hold my shaking body together. Goosebumps break out over my skin, yet sweat breaks out across my back. I can't seem to stop my leg from twitching wildly. I risk a glance and meet the detective's calm intelligent eyes, it's important that I get this right. It's essential, after all, I know that. I swallow my pain, it's a bitter, vile pill to have to stomach.

"So, it's your belief he killed those girls?" The detective asks.

He has a deep velvety voice with a richness hidden within the tones that I find I quite like. I see his wedding ring, still sparkly and new on his finger. I wonder what his wife, or maybe his husband, thinks of his long, unsociable hours. Does he love that person as much as he did when he married them? Or is one of those people already regretting the vows and promises they made together?

I take a deep, shuddering breath and answer.

"Yes, Detective, I suppose it must be true. After all, whoever knows a person really? I had no idea he killed those girls at the time. I mean, how could I? They were so nice and full of fun. I was happy to make friends with them both. It was lonely out there. I thought they'd just left and not told me, I mean, us. As for your earlier question, he ran, I think. They ran off together to hide. Him and her. It hurts so much. To be deceived like that and then to find out that I married a killer. It's unbelievable, really it is. He was an angry man, you know, deep down. My parents died, one after the other. I was so vulnerable when I met him and maybe a little weak, too. That's how he tricked me so badly. That's how he found his way in. I'm so angry at myself, detective. I should have seen, I should have noticed. If I had, innocent people wouldn't have died. He stole my money too, well, they did. They took it all."

The detective smiles at me, a smile laced with pity and sadness. I feel my stomach untwist only slightly, but it loosens all the same.

"People like him, they're very clever. It's not your fault in any way at all," he tells me. "We'll find him. Mexico, did you say?"

"Yes, he always wanted to see Mexico, I imagine that's where they went. Together."

He nods and shuffles his paperwork. I sense our meeting has come to an end, the detective has lots to do, because of me.

I did well, I tell myself, *I did really well.*

I stand and shake the detective's damp hand. All I want to do is go home. Go home to lick my wounds and curl myself into a ball. Maybe have a sandwich or something good to eat for comfort.

The worse parts are over now and he believes you. The tall, handsome detective believes every word you just said. Everything is going to be okay.

I smile as I leave. A small hidden smile that, of course, no one can see.

What a shame it was all nothing but lies.

Now for the truth, a secret to hold, just for you.

I suppose it all started the first moment I saw him. After all, who was I before him? I can't recall much of myself from before.

I worked for my father in the butcher store he owned. I spent my days and evenings chopping and bagging meats and washing the blood from the floors.

I was never squeamish, I grew used to the gore, so much so that I had, in fact, planned to be a mortuary assistant someday. Death in its many forms always fascinated me.

As it happened, my mother died. She keeled over quite dramatically while she caught the latest episode of the show she loved, knitting pins firmly gripped in her hand.

Before my mother turned cold in her eternal box, I took her place at the front of the store.

Now, one thing people never seemed to realize about me is this: I lacked emotional depth entirely.

I acted as if I possessed such a skill, of course, I did. But it had eluded me from day one. I imagined feelings to be great wild bursts of color, while I was a plain and standard gray. Real genuine feelings became something out of my reach entirely.

I watched people from a young age and so I learned how to play at one correctly. I managed to become the perfect mimic and I was good at it too.

From time to time, I received an odd look from one of our customers and I would understand from their frowns or expressions that I'd messed up. The older I got, the rarer those looks became. My people mask stayed firmly glued in its place. I became known as a kind and quiet girl. A nice girl.

I was, I guess am, a psychopath by definition. I just didn't know early on and for me, it was never really that straightforward to begin with.

My father began to irritate me soon after my mother died, so I poisoned him.

I made the decision and I stuck to it. Nobody suspected the grieving daughter, me, with my kind, pretty face, and sweetness. I had no regrets, it was simply his time to go.

I always loved control.

Town rumor had it that my father died of a broken heart, on account of my mother's death and the butcher store became mine.

Three days after my father's funeral, after my fake tears and the gentle dab at my dry eyes in public, he walked in.

Him, my life. The man that would turn my dull empty world into a whole new universe, one full of splashes of vibrancy and colors unknown.

"I'm looking for cuts of steak, please," he said.

Unromantic, I know.

I simply stared.

His face looked chiseled in that perfect definition of classical beauty that some people are lucky enough to be gifted. His blue eyes sparkled and he had the tiny beginnings of wrinkles in the corners. He was tall, taller than me, and walked with a grace I wouldn't dare to even try to copy.

My words escaped me entirely.

"A steak, please? Well, two actually," he prompted me.

"What for?" I said.

I was aware that I was blinking rapidly while my brain ran haywire by itself. I could picture us both living in a farmhouse, somewhere rural maybe. With a litter of blonde-haired children scampering around while I placed washing out on a line, one he'd hung with his strong, muscular arms.

"For me," he smiled and revealed perfect white teeth. A look of confusion swept across his features as he took an unconscious step back.

"I'm sorry," I beamed. "I simply meant to ask what the occasion might be? We have various types of steak, different quality, and different prices, you see."

"Ah, well, I have a date."

Tornadoes themselves whirled around inside of me. Thunder and lightning shattered me in two. I reminded myself to breathe and conjured up my most effective charm act.

"Then she's a lucky girl. I'll fetch our best then, shall I?"

He grinned and nodded. I went out back and picked up two of the worst steaks I could find. Ones that had been destined for the bin.

Before I wrapped them, I threw them both on the floor first. I was overwhelmed with rage and jealousy right then and I didn't even know his name. I pulled my apron lower and opened a few of my shirt buttons.

"Here you are. I hope your date goes well," I lied.

He met my eyes and paused. I had a feeling he was on the cusp of saying something important to me but thought he better of it.

"Are you okay?" I asked and tried to prompt him.

He took an awkward, almost clumsy step forward, and his beautiful mouth spoke. "I just realized. You're the girl whose parents both died recently, aren't you? News travels fast in this town."

"I am, yes, and it's been hard. I'm on my own, you see. It's just me."

I fluttered my eyelashes, a look I copied from the movies.

"I get lonely," I added. "So lonely."

"Sorry for you. That's really tough. Say, maybe we can get coffee sometime. If you'd like that?"

Oh yes, I very much did like that.

That was the beginning. My true beginning in my gray life. My own personal rebirth. I was obsessed.

His hair smelt permanently of baby powder and the lemon shower gel he always preferred to use. His hands were both soft and firm at the very same time and that smile he saved for when he felt truly happy, thrilled me.

He made me feel emotions that were brand new. A whole explosion of clarity and colorful feelings. One coffee turned into two, and on and on. Six months later, he moved into my apartment above the butcher store. Two months after that, he asked me to marry him.

He actually bent down on one knee and asked me. Of course, I said yes. I was deliriously happy. I'd won, after all. My act cracked slightly over the course of our time together. But the cracks themselves were hairline fractures and hardly noticeable from the outside.

Truly, I deserved an Oscar for my performance.

It was on our honeymoon, hiking in a national park, when our relationship took the nastiest of blows.

That's where I first killed someone. At least, the first one he knew of.

I probably need to backtrack. I get ahead of myself sometimes. I often think that my mind might keep its memories safe and locked away on records. Old black spinning records, the type that was popular years ago. I have to go off and retrieve them from the dusty boxes in the corners of my mind and dust them down, or they won't play again. Sometimes my memories are too scratched and when I try to play them, parts skip by mistake or refuse to play at all.

So, to the best of my knowledge, the sequence of events was as follows.

In blissful happiness, we were eight days into a ten-day hiking adventure. Nothing but lush trees and dogged trails, walking, and romantic nights under the stars. He had chosen the national park as our destination. Him.

We made love every night and it was me that became the insatiable one. I felt forever hungry for him. In the daytime, while he hiked ahead of me, I stopped to watch him move until he had to shout my name and tell me to catch up.

On the eighth day, lost in our own private world and after seeing nobody around for days, we bumped into two girls who were hiking together. By girls I mean, younger than me and with breasts much perkier than mine. Obviously, I hated them.

I saw him stare at their chests first, while I held their eyes. I suppose that's quite normal for a man, it's what they do when they get confronted by young beauty, after all. But I didn't like it, not one bit.

My veins filled up with the curious feeling of ice, that awful coldness that seeps in so hard you feel as if liquid nitrogen were running amok inside the marrow of your bones.

I elbowed him roughly as the girls smiled their wide, perfect toothed grins.

"How's your hike, ladies?" I said, while my heartbeat thundered in my ears.

"Great! We're camping by the river tonight."

"So are we!" my husband exclaimed.

"No darling, we're carrying on remember, a few more miles yet," I snarled and tried to keep the fake grin plastered on my face.

"We have beers, come and join us!" One of the girls said.

She had an accent from an Icelandic-type country and that made me hate her even more. Her voice sounded alluring and joyfully young.

I knew then that I was losing control of the situation and I never did like to lose.

"We just got married," I reminded him. "We came here for privacy."

Those two were so bubbly that it made me sick all the way inside. They acted as if life had been a breeze so far, and I hated that.

No doubt they both had bright futures ahead, lives with no real issues to face.

I pictured them both as an older woman, stuck in the gilded cages of a vast empty home, alone with their prescription pills and martinis while their husbands were off with younger versions of them. A cliché, I know, but those girls were a cliché too.

"I'm sure we can camp one night," he said. "It'll be fun."

I stalked off to the water. I always liked to look at currents running, all that power and force running by energies unknown to me. I felt the same way inside every day.

We did camp. I wasn't really given the choice. He set up our tent not far from theirs and ignored my protests.

The girls both made a show of dragging over fallen logs to use as seats and one of them even dug a fire pit, although she giggled the whole time. The three of them talked about his job as a schoolteacher and their future jobs as wives of doctors and lawyers or some such.

I wasn't listening. I was sulking.

"Join in," he told me. "Lighten up."

Indeed.

A ball of rage began to grow. It spread its tendrils out from my heart and overtook me. As night began to fall, he lit the fire in that manly way of his. The girls passed around a bottle of whiskey and danced, without any regard for me, the wife who watched gloomily from a distance. He stared at them with the greediest of expressions as they flirted. How I hated him in those moments.

Imagine his horror and surprise when I shot them both.

I'd owned the gun for a while. I brought it all quite legally when I first took ownership of the store and I knew how to shoot and how to shoot well. We do indeed live in dangerous times and I wanted to protect myself and then later, him too.

When he'd suggested hiking, I started to worry about bears, so I brought it along. I didn't want his perfect, beautiful face to be ruined and mauled by a giant furry claw, I enjoyed looking at it far too much. I regarded his face as my face. Mine.

From the day I met him, he became everything to me. My reason to live and my anchor to the world. One that had a tight and small chain that I fashioned to be that way. I decided he wasn't allowed to look at anyone other than me in that hungry way of his.

You might wonder why I shot the girls when, really, it was his disrespect. But isn't it always the way with women, that we blame the females more than the men?

The power and force of those shots almost knocked me off my feet.

"What the hell!" He wailed.

He staggered back as if I were the monster and not the girls. His face was patterned with splashes of crimson.

"What do you expect!" I raged. "You were practically cumming all over them both. How dare you! You belong to me now! WE ARE MARRIED."

The end of my sentence boomed throughout the forest, a show of my betrayal and fury. My hands shook and I aimed the gun at him.

"Dare to run and I'll shoot you too," I screamed.

Tears ran down his face and his mouth kept bobbing open like a little fish taken straight from the water.

"Oh my God, oh my God, oh my God," he chanted while spit ran down his face.

"Get a grip darling," I growled.

We sat in absolute silence. I let him wail and cry, I let him shake and sob. All I could hear was the sound of the water and a gentle breeze that swayed the trees.

"I love you," I eventually said.

"Why would you kill them? They did nothing wrong. You have no right."

"Yes I do," I told him because I did, I did have the right.

"You belong to me. You said you loved me. You made a vow," I added.

One of the girls chose that moment to splutter and cough blood high in the air. She gurgled and opened her eyes. Her bewildered, glassy gaze landed on me.

"Oh shit," I said.

"Listen, put the gun on the ground. I'll go and get help."

"No."

"Please, I'm asking you as your husband."

"No."

He had the absurd nerve to raise his arms as if I were the bad guy in the situation and holding him hostage.

I stared at him, his face soothed my soul and his expression made me want to laugh.

"I'm sorry," I told him. "I really am. Will you help me?"

The girl moaned in pain, I ignored her and walked towards him.

"There's a darkness in me," I said. "Help me get rid of it. I love you so much, that's all."

"You're asking me to cover up a double murder for you?"

"Yes."

"No."

"Then I'll shoot us both."

"No, you won't."

"I will actually."

"Okay, okay, I'll do it. I'll help you."

The backstabbing piece of shit did help me. He helped me so much he practically did everything. We dug graves for the bodies. By the time we'd finished, the girl had died anyway. I didn't even see it happen, which was a shame. I'd wanted to look her in the eye and smile. I'd won again, you see. If life was a game, I was in first place and he was still mine. Him, just for me.

The next two days were awkward, and I refused to let him out of my sight as we made our way back out of the park. He did not appreciate this, he wanted privacy to use the toilet and I wouldn't let him.

"Did you enjoy killing them?" He asked me.

"No, but they deserved it."

"Have you killed before?"

"Of course not," I lied. "I was overcome with emotion. Because I love you."

He hadn't replied.

The nights in our tent were brutal. He turned away from me and one night all he even did was cry. I thought then that he was just upset because he loved me so much.

"Help me, I can make it right. We can put it behind us."

"I won't be able to," he stated. "You're unstable."

"If you tell anyone or leave me, I'll kill you."

I said that because it was true. Because I was terrified beyond words and I didn't like the feeling at all. I wasn't bothered about prison or being punished for my crime. I only cared that prison would take me away from him, and I couldn't allow that to happen. I felt the chain on my anchor, our tie that binds, loosen a little, and it scared me.

"I'll do anything you want. I can change," I begged.

"Go to sleep."

We got back to our car, the car I bought for him, and we drove home in silence. He refused to speak to me for the entire hundred or so miles.

As soon as we got home, he went straight to bed.

I went online and ordered a tracking device for his car. I canceled his phone service and set up a brand new one in my name, one I had full access to. I watched him sleep, I watched him pretend to be asleep.

I cooked a casserole, his favorite kind, and I took it into our room, into our marital bedroom, and served it on a special tray just for him.

"I don't know who you are anymore," he said.

"I'm your wife, darling. For better or for worse."

"We should get an annulment, a divorce. It was a mistake. I'm sorry. I won't tell a soul what you did. I promise."

"What *we* did you mean."

"No, you."

"No, darling. You," I told him. "Your DNA will be on those bodies, not mine. You fired the gun. Not me, at least, that's what I'll tell anyone who happens to ask. While you were busy digging graves, I emptied your hairbrush of hair. Both girls got a handful as if there'd been a fight. Your mouth guard, that silly plastic contraption you wear? I wiped it all over them, and who'd ever believe that I was a killer?"

"You're crazy. You're mad."

"I'm going to call a friend and say you were acting a little odd for those last few days. I'll say we met two girls and you argued with them. I'm planting seeds, darling, and you and I both know seeds grow. Now, call the police, I dare you."

"You're a psycho."

"No, I'm your wife. Till death do us part. Remember, darling?"

I suppose you can imagine that the next few weeks were tough. I wore my best, most charming mask and I wore my very best act.

He refused to touch me and it hurt.

I worked in the butcher store every day, I smiled and I asked how everyone was. I made an effort in every single thing I did. I made a few comments to people I knew, I said he was acting strange and angry. I said I was concerned about him.

I made an effort with him, a big effort.

I cooked, cleaned, washed, and ironed. I played at the perfect housewife every evening. Little by little, he relaxed. At least, I thought he had.

It's working, I told myself. *It's definitely working.*

I watched his car on my laptop, that little red dot going to and from the school he worked at. I monitored his calls. I watched him and I waited. Almost every day I expected police to be knocking at the door or tearing it down. Every night I breathed a sigh of relief as he seemed to thaw a little more.

One morning, a Tuesday in fact, he told me he was going for drinks with his teacher friends after school. I felt the dagger hanging over my head fall down closer and tilt a little.

"Of course," I smiled through gritted teeth. "Can I come along too?"

"It's just for teachers," he said. "Just for faculty and you wouldn't enjoy it."

Thoughts twisted around in my mind all day while different scenarios tumbled over one another. I closed the store early and fled upstairs.

I watched the little red dot of his car blip into action. I watched its progress along streets and roads until it stopped in front of a smart row of newly built apartments. The scene of my betrayal.

I dressed in black clothing and left. But not before I tucked one of my sharpest knives into the deep pockets of my coat.

It was dark by the time I arrived on foot. With each step I took to get there, the rage came back full force and spiraled its way out of control. I plotted and I fumed, I planned and I boiled inside.

I hadn't known what I expected to find. Not really.

But I already knew that somehow, the man that had set my word ablaze was betraying me, the pain felt exquisitely sharp and brutal. I was hungry, deep down inside for revenge before I even approached the apartment block.

Fate decided my future, or at least made it easier to witness my decline.

A single downstairs apartment was lit up and the blind was only half drawn. I peered inside slowly. My husband, my love, my whole life. He was sitting at a flimsy, cheap kitchen table with a brunette woman. He held his head in his hands as she stared at him, with her hand placed over her pretty mouth.

She reached out and laid a hand on his shoulder. Vomit rose in my throat as I fought the bitterness back down. That was my shoulder, only I was allowed to touch it.

I knew he was telling her my secrets, our secret, and I knew who she was. The pretty girl from the flower store a few doors down from mine. The one he dated before me. The girl I stole him from although he was mine, he was always mine.

My hand clasped the hilt of the knife inside my coat. In a single second, I decided to press the bell and confront them both.

But then an idea occurred to me and instead, I went home. I cried no tears on my solitary journey back, that skill had always been beyond me. Instead, I laughed at my own cunning.

When you learn what I did, you might understand why.

He came home and my act was already settled back in place. I rubbed his tense shoulders for him as he grimaced and I ignored the smell of whiskey and lies on his breath.

"Why did you do it?" He asked.

"It was a mistake, a glitch. I didn't mean to. I hate myself for it," I said.

Thick deafening silence settled between us and I leaned forward to smell his lemon and baby powder smell. He smelt of perfume instead. Her perfume, not mine.

"This can't go on," he told me.

"I know," I said. "It won't."

We were both talking about different things and I knew it. My perspective was not his anymore. He was a magnet for me and the polarity had switched.

He went to bed and lay down with his back to me like a slab of ice. I watched him all night. I watched the steady rise of his chest and I listened to the gentle sounds of his snores. My back felt full of daggers and knives, each one pierced my soul until it bled.

Him, he had destroyed us.

The next day, I sprang into action. I paced and planned. I shook with adrenaline as I dialed the flower store, the one the girl he'd been with worked at.

"Hi," I said in my most gentle and sweet voice. "I believe my husband has been telling you lies and setting me up. Please, could you spare ten minutes to hear my side? He's dangerous, you see, and I can prove it. I really can."

"I… umm…"

"I really can prove it."

"It wouldn't be appropriate," she told me.

"Please," I fake sobbed. "And come in the back way of my store, in case he's watching. Please, I beg you and don't tell anyone. If he finds out…"

It only took her fifteen minutes. Fifteen minutes for her curiosity to pique to overflowing, only nine hundred seconds for her to decide her own fate.

I listened for the bell around the back. The bell usually reserved for meat deliveries only. I closed the store briefly with a handwritten 'Back in ten' sign.

She stalked in and glanced around in her smart outfit and fancy shoes. I always kept the chopping and cutting areas extremely clean, all the same, she raised a perfect eyebrow in disgust as she sat very elegantly for a traitor, politely for a stealer of husbands.

I despised her, her with her pretty face and flowery scent. She stared at me and blinked rapidly. She was a demon to me, a demon in an outfit of skin and nasty clothing.

"First of all, before I tell you the truth about him, are you sleeping together?" I asked.

Her face reddened at my words and I knew the truth right then, although she shook her head.

"No," she said, but I saw the lust and memories in her eyes. I always know a liar when I see one. For a second, it amazed me how they'd even had the time to fuck or how they'd gotten in the mood in the first place after talking about me and what I'd done.

"He's going to leave you, you know. Any day now, he'll leave and go to the police. I know what you did, but he…"

A burst of adrenaline exploded inside me. My mask slipped and fell off entirely. I felt as if I'd been kicked in the stomach, the blow was so strong that I jolted and staggered back. Then came the rage,

Sarah Jane Huntington

the blackness. It flooded my system until I was nothing but a ball of fury. Electricity crackled and popped in my blood as I sprang for her, her, the enemy.

Her eyes widened in panic. She gasped and gurgled when I plunged my best sharp knife straight into her heart. Right in the very same place my own pain lived in and festered.

"He's mine," I seethed. "Mine."

The light behind her eyes faded as she died without any more sounds. Blood poured from her pretty mouth and I kicked her off my chair. She crashed to the floor on her face. I stamped on her head for good measure, I only felt bad that she couldn't feel it.

I fetched my biggest chopping knives, the good ones I keep aside for thick meats, and I got to work.

I removed the sign from the window and found a queue of two people, regulars, both waiting for me outside.

"That was a long ten minutes!" One said. "I've been waiting for an age!"

"I'm so sorry," I said. "I had a migraine. The stress, I think."

"Oh, dear, whatever is the matter?"

"My husband," I said. "I think he's seeing someone else. In fact, I'm

sure he is."

I wiped my face with a wet tissue for the illusion of tears. It was a trick I used for years.

My two kindly customers crooned and soothed. They both seemed genuinely concerned for me and I knew they'd go off and spread my troubles all around town and I was counting on it.

Every time the store emptied, I went out to the back to work. An hour or so later, the meat delivery came, and that made my task a lot easier and simpler.

By the time he came home, I had supper cooked and new white pillar candles lit at our dining table. I took his jacket and asked him about his day.

He shrugged and ignored me.

"Sit and eat," I told him. "Let's talk like a normal couple. I made your favorite casserole."

He sat in silence and I poured him a double whiskey. He drank it back in one and grimaced, so I poured him another, and then another.

"Eat," I prompted, and so he did.

112

He looked gaunt in the candlelight, only half the man he used to be. His blue eyes had lost their sparkle, his tiny wrinkles had deepened. His shirt hung loose on his thinning body and gray hairs poked out from the blonde. I watched him eat a few mouthfuls while several thoughts stampeded for the main position in my mind.

I truly thought that we had our whole lives to look forward to together. I guess I also knew that I wasn't the same as other people and no matter how hard I ever tried, I never would be.

So, I guess that abyss of difference was almost bound to trip me up at some point. Trip us up.

People like me are a fascination for some. They watch psychopaths or killers on the silver screen and they feel troubled or scared, but only for a short time. The evil for them is contained within a giant screen. The depraved, the deranged, and the dangerous exist for entertainment purposes only. Yet, for me, it is simply the way I am.

Those people go home and climb into their comfortable beds, maybe they worry about their jobs, or their bills, or their children. They don't expect a member of their own society to ever be a threat to them or their families. They don't expect a killer to be running their local butcher store, they don't expect that their wife or husband might well be wearing a real or a metaphorical human-shaped mask.

For them, there is grim voyeurism in watching fake blood-curdling screams and of seeing heads in boxes mailed to detectives by someone playing the most ancient and noble game of cat and mouse.

People like me, we feel, we do.

Pain, revenge, control, and instinct. But for me, I once felt love. The deliriously addictive emotion of love. One thing that can both build or destroy completely.

"I love you," I told him. "At least, I did."

"Huh?"

"Darling, how could you? Wasn't I the perfect wife?"

He stared at me and in that cold look, I saw hate, real genuine despair, and hate.

"What? You're a murderer, and you've trapped me. You make me sick. You only play at being a perfect wife! None of it's real, is it!?"

A bubble of anger burned in my chest. How dare he? After all, I did for him. A little flutter of butterflies started up in my stomach. I held my laughter inside and reminded myself of control.

"Is that why you want to leave me for her?" I said.

"I don't know what you're talking about," he snapped. He lied.

"I know, darling, I know all about it. In fact, she was here earlier. Your girlfriend, the mistress, she was here."

His spoon froze on the way to his mouth, he dropped it as if it were red hot and it clattered loudly into his empty, almost licked clean bowl.

"What have you done? Where is she?" Spit flew from his mouth and settled on the table.

"She's part of you now, isn't that what you always wanted? Darling."

"You're mad. Where is she? Pass me my phone."

"She's in the casserole. You just ate her. You ate her all up!"

I couldn't help it any longer. I laughed a manic laugh.

I smiled a smile of absolute triumph as I watched his features show a range of expressions that made me quite jealous of their realism. How I wished I could show emotions that way, I tucked them away for future use, certain they might come in handy.

I expected him to turn and vomit, or maybe stick his fingers down his throat. Instead, he surprised me and made a grab for me. His chair crashed to the floor as he tried to dash around the table. The pills I'd put in his whiskey slowed him down just enough and he fell to the floor in a tangle. I crouched down low so I could be with him.

"What a fool you are. You had it all," I reminded him.

"Stop this, please," he croaked. I recognized his expression as fear, and I stroked his hair to soothe him. Even though everything was his fault, I could still play at being kind.

"If I can't have you…." I whispered into his ear. "Nobody can."

I slit his throat.

It pained me to have to do that. It hurt me to know that he'd given me no choice or any alternative.

I held him as he died, I wrapped my arms around him as the spark inside him drained away. It happened quicker than I expected.

I dragged his body downstairs and the clean-up took all night.

In the morning I called a friend, one I kept in touch with in case I ever needed her for anything, and I told her that I woke up to find him gone. I said he'd taken all of our money, all the cash I'd been saving in the house. I said I was hurt, I said I was in pain and that it was relentless. That part, at least, was true.

Later that day, I held a sale of fresh meat and I had lots of eager and happy customers.

"I had a good meat deal, a really good one," I told everyone. "And it's only fair to share it, after all, you've all been so kind."

Customers left with bags full and everyone was pleased. Scraps went into the furnace and I watched the fire burn them all. I've always liked fire. It's one of my most favorite things to look at.

The next day, people came back wanting more meat.

"Those sausages were delicious!" And, "that pork went down a treat!" were just a couple of the compliments I received.

A day later, I reported my husband as an official missing person. I told an officer that I suspected he'd been having an affair with someone local and that they'd taken my money and fled. Possibly to Mexico.

I received sympathy all around. Rumor had it that a young woman was also missing, a local woman from the flower store. The town put two and two together until it became a fact that the pair had run away together.

That piece of gossip suited me just fine.

My business was booming and it kept me extremely busy. It was in the evenings when I missed him deeply. I told myself that it was better to have loved and lost than never to have loved before. But the pain still settled on my chest like an enormous boulder that I couldn't shift.

The color in the world died for me and life returned to a standard gray.

Then, two female bodies were found in the same national park we hiked in for our honeymoon. My friend called to tell me, she whispered to me and asked if it was possible that he might have done something terrible to those girls.

"Yes," I told her, "It's very possible that he did just that."

I arranged my face into a copied expression of shock and made my way to the police station to report my nagging suspicions.

His legacy soon came to be that he was a murderer on the run from the authorities. A double killer, no less. A schoolteacher, a thief, and an adulterer. No one suspected me. Not once.

I loved him dearly, I did. I keep a few thin slices of him in my own personal freezer. When the pain becomes too much, I make a sandwich. He stays close to me that way. He's always with me.

As quickly as the love started up, it stopped. He shattered it. He did. Broken things never quite look the same as they do when they're new. You can always notice the crack, or a chunk missing here and there, if you happen to look hard enough. Others notice too, they sense a chip or fault in something that used to be beautiful. They know if there's a weakness, a soft piece of scarring, or a way in.

It was his fault. We made vows that only took him just eight days to break. Only eight days.

How can I be to blame? I only operate on instinct, after all. There is no desire to cause suffering planted deep within my warped DNA. There is no button to switch, no code to activate the drive of a killer. No bare wiring that sparks together in the wrong places. I was a woman in love. More in love than fairy tales talk of, or myths and legends say. More in love than wandering minstrels sang of long ago. More in love than I could stand.

It was him that pulled too hard on our bindings. Him that twisted and warped our sacred bond. My survival instinct drew itself tall and protected me. If I let him walk away, let him leave me behind, all broken with his betrayal, then how would I have lived? Who was I before him, after all?

It's my nature, that's all. My instinct to survive.

My friends, you know what they say about a woman scorned.

And after all, I'm just a nice and quiet girl.

A DIFFERENT KIND OF RAIN

Everyone left has a story, their very own tale, from when it happened. Stories of where they were when they first heard and how they felt.

This is mine.

Lots of people, all different kinds of people and from all walks of life, said that they came in the rain.

Scientists in fancy white coats said it, ones that had pens and pencils they never used sticking uselessly up out of their pockets. Solemn yet excited news presenters said it, with their collagen plumped lips, orange tans, and brightly whitened teeth. Most importantly of all, the only known survivor and witness of 'The Event' said it.

The Event, that's what they called it.

Two simple effective words were placed together and everyone knew exactly what they meant. Those two words became known in every language in the world. I doubted there was a soul in existence who failed to know the meaning.

"It was a one-off," the Government assured.

"The event was contained," the scientists told us.

"No doubt it came from space," an astronomer said.

"No, no," argued a physicist. "Another dimension is the answer."

I didn't believe them. None of them.

The Event first occurred in India, within a small inhabited village set close to the ocean. Rumor was that villagers themselves had been praying hard for rain. They got their wish, I suppose, just not the kind they asked for.

Blood-colored rain began to fall as night drew near on a pleasant Sunday evening. By morning, sixty villagers were affected, or maybe it should have been afflicted. One eight-year-old child ran away and hid before the rain even had itself the idea to fall. The child saw animals scamper away, he watched the birds leave in a sudden flurry and he'd seen the great effort even the insects made in fleeing.

The clever boy copied them all and ran.

"It's a contagion," they said. One unknown to our most clever scientists.

Amateur footage spread across the internet faster than it could be deleted.

Shaky videos showed bodies lying quarantined and cocooned on the dry, harsh ground. Each one lay wrapped in what looked like a red thread, or sometimes the texture mimicked bright red wool, depending upon the light or particular angle.

"It'll happen again," I told my sometimes, on-off boyfriend Jake.

"They said it won't," he answered. "They know."

They.

They said this, they said that. Who are those 'They?' The fabled great ones that always seemed to know everything?

"It will. Wait and see," I said.

As it turned out, I was right and I didn't feel smug about it one bit. It did happen again and then again and again. Blood red rain struck New York City at four in the afternoon on a bright sunny day.

The casualties numbered in the thousands. Individuals became a number, each one wrapped head to toe in red thread.

A chrysalis, a human one.

Within hours, rioting began. Highways became grid locked as people fled. Suicides skyrocketed, looters swarmed, and the economy crashed.

I watched it unfold via my television in my high up apartment. By twenty-twenty, we humans had become used to natural disasters. We were desensitized to mass casualty events and an old hand at contagions.

The Event was different, the whole world stopped to watch in absolute horror, for once united in a global and shocking threat.

Red rain fell on London only hours after New York had been decimated. Footage showed those walking outside pat at themselves in confusion as the red rain fell. Within seconds, there was a mass cry of outraged and frightened screams.

A close-up showed one drop of rain explode on a smartly dressed businesswoman. The drop grew with thick tendrils, tentacles, as if they'd been conjured up out of thin air. Those tendrils erupted and bound an entire person in less than twenty seconds. Slow-motion made it look as if a human was being greedily devoured by an otherworldly octopus. Of course, they weren't, but it looked that way to me all the same.

New stations buzzed with both terror and excitement. Theories raced around the internet. No one knew what became of those inside the cocoons, that bothered me a lot and I mean, a lot. I watched the scenes unfold as if I were binge-watching a new Netflix series. At times, I had to remind myself it was real. An earth-wide horror reality show.

"Maybe they turn to mush inside? Transform somehow, just like caterpillars do?" I suggested to Jake.

"I don't know," he shrugged. "Maybe."

"They might be brand new after, I mean, what's the point of red rain wrapping these people up? What's its purpose? Are they even alive in there?"

"I don't know," he said.

Jake didn't know a lot.

Those were questions everyone wanted and demanded to know. In the hours that followed both New York and London's events, sheer panic erupted.

Curfews were announced that no one followed. People were deeply afraid and it showed. Congress was surrounded by an angry mob, those inside barricaded themselves in. Others chose to riot outside the Whitehouse as if it were all the President's fault.

It wasn't the same as watching some disaster in a faraway country, one a person could donate money to and then post that they had on social media for the likes. People soon realized that this terror might well affect them personally and that made all the difference.

Almost everyone became an armchair expert, an angry, frightened fake news spreading conspiracy theorist.

Hashtags blamed the Deep State, the CIA, MI5, Aliens, HAARP, even terrorists.

One particular hashtag even blamed ghosts.

Our president stuttered his way through a live speech that was meant to unite, he failed and fled into hiding while martial law was declared.

Military jets flew overhead, and tanks patrolled our angry mobbed streets. Sirens sounded at obscure hours, as if a massive storm front was incoming, which, in a way, I suppose it was.

I was extremely frightened for myself, of course, and for others too.

Gunfire broke up the rare moments of silence in the night, every night. I didn't sleep much, curiosity had me too afraid to miss anything, nor did I dare to leave my apartment.

The world watched as people in biohazard suits collected the people cocoons. They were placed delicately together into the backs of army vehicles, loaded up and taken away. Still, cocoons littered the streets in the hundreds.

Someone, nobody knows who, shot at one. The bullet bounced off as if the red thread was metallic, it even made that distinctive clang sound. Police officers had to guard the rest, they stood warily by, hands-on guns until the rest of the cocoons were collected.

A smart looking man on a special television panel wondered aloud if the rain might have come falling down from an infected meteorite. Another wondered if CERN had opened a doorway to another universe, either by design or mistake.

CERN themselves pleaded ignorance.

"They play with the fabric of the universe itself!" The smart man wailed.

"It might be the fault of a quantum computer, they can exchange information with other realms, you know," a smug woman said.

"You're all wrong, it's a new contagion. Or biological warfare," a CDC spokesperson announced.

Religious figures called the rain Wormwood and said it was God's second flood, sent to punish us, his most unworthy children. They called New York, Babylon, and said it had fallen.

"It is a judgment," a well-known and very wealthy minister proclaimed from his mansion. "God has seen us and found us to be lacking. It is the red horse of Revelations!"

A popular Christian author spoke live on the news.

"Sodom and Gomorrah fell!" He shouted, "The gays caused this, the lesbians and their abhorrent behavior!"

He was so enraged, he had to be dragged off-screen by security with his feet kicking the air as he went. His opinions were so ridiculous and awful, he made me wish he were one of the cocooned.

People screamed that it was the end of the world, some even wore sandwich boards proclaiming the 'END IS NIGH,' and wandered the streets. Others waited for their messiah or an antichrist to make an appearance.

One young activist blamed humans.

"Mother nature has had enough. We are the parasites," she said.

I felt inclined to agree.

I watched television day and night, and I waited. I searched the internet, I read every theory. I hoped the dead had found their peace, if they were, in fact, dead.

No more rain fell and a month passed slowly. Everyone began to believe it might be over. Event one, two, and three were spoken of in the past tense.

People began to ask, "Where were you when it happened?"

Personal stories started to spread.

'My mother was cocooned,' and 'Daddy is a chrysalis,' were both the headlines of national newspapers as people began to cash in on their losses.

Others flocked to churches and temples. Cults started up and collected hundreds of members a day.

"We have been given an opportunity to change," the Pope announced from his balcony in Rome. "A second chance at our redemption. This was a warning."

Religious figures around the world held hands in a televised show of faith, they prayed together and prayed for the souls that had been lost.

Irrelevant singers held out of tune concerts in memory of those gone.

I sat and watched, and I hoped the world was right, I hoped it was over.

People returned to the sad rhythm of their normal lives. Schools reopened, curfews were lifted. The president poked his grey head out of the hole he'd been hiding in and thanked God for the reprieve. Bunkers opened. Weapons were laid down, militia groups relaxed.

Then.

Well, then the cocoons opened and things really got bad.

* * *

Jake had left for his own home weeks before and I hadn't even thought of him in the entire time he'd been gone. I had a feeling in the pit of my stomach that The Event wasn't over. Not by a long shot.

I believed it had only been act one in a long, brutal play.

As soon as the stores opened up, I left the safety of my apartment and went to stock up on canned goods and dried pasta. I even brought a camping stove with extra gas after watching a prepper channel on YouTube.

I watched the news for almost twenty-four hours a day and I waited. I was lurking around on a forum dedicated to solving The Event when a new thread popped up. 'Urgent,' it said. 'Very urgent.'

The author of the post claimed to be working for the CDC. He said that the cocoons had refused to be opened, no matter which method they tried. Even X-ray scans failed to detect what might be happening inside. The person, the whistleblower, then went on to say that at exactly two that morning, they had begun to open all by themselves.

No sooner had the thread been posted, than a flurry of replies hit. Every member wanted proof, and everyone craved to know what was inside.

The whistleblower hadn't known. The vast area the cocoons were stored in had been quickly evacuated.

I felt curious but not convinced, after all, anyone could post any- thing and it might not be true at all. I kept the information in my mind as something to think about sometime.

I curled up on my sofa, muted the news, and I slept.

When I woke up, it was dark outside. I stretched and opened one eye to peer at my television.

I can perfectly recall the jolt of terror that rushed through me like an electric shock. I sat up, eyes wide and with my mouth hanging open. Heavy bangs and loud voices came from the apartment above me as I stared at my screen.

The television played an alert over and over, one that said to seek immediate shelter, as if a tornado were inbound. Outside, I heard two gunshots and a scream of high-pitched desperation.

My stomach dropped and I fought off a wave of panic. I vowed to stay calm, but I had no real idea of what I should do. Another scream met my ears and I heard a helicopter in the distance. One of those big double-bladed ones that sound like 'whomp, whomp, whomp' and mean serious business.

I ran to my window and peered down onto the street below.

I dropped down and vomited as soon as I got a clear look. On my hands and knees, I crawled until I was tucked under my small wooden table. I tried harder than I ever have before to keep a grip on my mind. My own sanity split apart at the edges.

"It's not real, I'm dreaming," I chanted and told myself, although I knew that my own words were nothing more than a warm and comfortable lie.

"Kelly!" someone yelled as pounding started up at my apartment door. I screamed in terror, although I knew the voice and it took me a long moment to realize it was my own name being shouted.

"Kelly, let me in!" The door handle jolted up and down, up and down. I sat and stared. I hadn't been able to move, not one inch. Looking back, I guess it was shock that had hold of me.

I heard keys jingle and I briefly wondered if the chain was on. Then I found myself looking into Jake's eyes as he shook me. I don't recall watching him cross the room towards me, my mind must have glitched as it tried to process exactly what it was I saw in the street.

"They're everywhere," he yelled and threw his hands into the air.

I think someone whined and it must have been me.

"Kelly, Kelly. It's me, you're okay," Jake soothed.

The image of those things filled my brain. Stuff like that isn't meant to exist outside of books or movies.

"Kelly?" Jake shouted and shook me again.

"What are they?" I hissed. Saliva fell from my mouth and I didn't even have the sense to wipe it away.

Pins and needles were running rampant all over my skin and I felt cold all the way inside myself.

Jake pulled me out from under the table even though I squealed in protest. He picked me up and dropped me back onto my sofa. His mouth moved and formed words, but I couldn't tell what they were.

My own heartbeat thundered in my ears and canceled any other sounds out until I felt as if I were deep underwater.

He disappeared, and then, in an instant, he was back. He pushed a hot drink into my hands and the situation turned surreal. I couldn't fathom why we were drinking hot tea while those things were running around outside.

My hands shook as I brought the mug up to my mouth. I wondered if I'd forgotten how to swallow and the tea ran down my chin.

My heartbeat calmed as Jake waited patiently.

"I thought you'd know already," he said. "You always know before me, all of this I mean."

"I sleep," I said. I shivered and tried again. "I was asleep, I mean."

He nodded, stood, and began to pace.

"Drink your tea, we have to get out of the city," he said.

"I'm not. I'm not going. What happened?"

"They opened Kelly, the news said the cocoons opened. Everything went off the air not long after. No cell signal, no service. The military is on the streets, jets, police, groups of people armed. No one knows what to do. It's a war. We're at war."

"We should stay."

"No, we don't stand a chance."

My brain glitched again and I refused to believe that. It seemed impossible. We were a superpower in the world, an unstoppable force to be reckoned with. How could it be that we wouldn't stand a chance?

"Why didn't you leave then?"

"'Cause of you, here on your own."

"Oh."

I suppose, until that point, I always saw Jake as a temporary fix. Someone that came into my life that I wouldn't be bothered about when they upped and left again. He was a person who took the edge off my existence.

I guessed we hadn't had the same views at all. I only gave him a key because I got tired of getting up to open the door for him.

"Someone said there's a safe haven in Alaska."

"It's too cold there," I answered. "I'm not going."

"For fuck's sake Kelly. We're not making holiday plans! Wake up!"

I started to cry then, big wracking sobs that shook my body. I wasn't crying for myself or for Jake. I was crying because our comfortable life was gone. The world as we knew it had ceased to exist and nothing, not one thing, would ever be the same.

I had no family left, they were all wiped out in a single accident years before. I'd been on my own for four years, so I knew a little about what survival truly meant. You had to keep breathing and keep going, no matter what the cost.

"We should hole up here, I have food," I sobbed. "I got prepared. The YouTube video said to do it."

"What if they nuke the city?"

"Will they?"

"I don't know, I mean, maybe. I would."

"That's awful, and Alaska is a hell of a long way, Jake."

"My dad still lives at the farm, remember? We could head there instead."

"We'll die trying," I said.

"We'll die if we don't."

I tried to think, to check inside myself and test if I had the courage to make the journey, or at least, try and make it.

I had never regarded myself as brave before. I never regarded myself as much of anything. I went through life being fairly invisible, and that suited me just fine. I had a part-time job I tolerated and a few friends that tolerated me.

"Someone said they can only see movement, the things I mean," Jake said.

"Like in Jurassic park?"

"What? That's absurd!"

"The T-Rex. It only knows you're there if you move. I don't know about smells or sounds. I forgot if T-Rex can…"

"Okay," Jake snapped. "I guess it is like a T-Rex, then. A guy I met on the way over, he had a gun, a shotgun. He said they can only get you if you move and that they can't smell or hear you."

I wanted to think about that, but our darkened room turned a faint amber as an explosion ripped through the night.

The boom shook the whole building. Orange and yellow shades lit up the room and made intricate patterns on the backs of my eyelids.

"Gas station, I'll bet," Jake announced. He crawled over to the window and peeked out. "Street looks pretty empty right now, none of those…things. The explosion was a block away, maybe."

"Can we go in the morning? Leave then I mean?" I whispered.

"We need to go now, pack a small bag, okay? You said you have food?"

I pointed to the cupboards in the kitchen and headed into my bedroom. My legs felt like strings of rubber, and I fell on my bed and took a few deep breaths. I took out a bag and added a few sweaters and jeans. I took my first aid kit and remembered my gun.

It had been my father's, and I hoped it could still fire. I had no idea how it worked, but I had spare bullets, too.

"Cool!" Jake said, visibly happier when I showed him. "I didn't know you had one!"

I stayed silent. I didn't tell him I'd been saving it for myself. Saving it for when life became too bad. The gun had been my source of comfort, my way out if I ever needed it. Sometimes I took it out and touched the cool metal. I'd tell myself I had to keep surviving and keep breathing. No matter what the cost.

Jake crammed a bag with pasta, a saucepan, and my new camping stove.

I took a look around my tiny apartment and knew I'd never likely see it again. It hadn't been a home for me, it was just a place to live, but I felt safe there, at least.

"We have to go, Kelly, you know that, don't you?"

"Yes," I said because I knew he was right and the government dropped nukes on civilians all the time in the movies.

"Come on then, before I change my mind."

"It'll be okay, the streets are probably empty of them, the military must be holding them back. It'll be a walk in the park."

Famous last words.

The first body was jammed in the elevator downstairs. We used the stairs anyway, in case the emergency power went out. We walked quietly and quickly until I saw the body. I think it was the lady that sometimes smiled at me if we happened to be in the basement laundry room at the same time, who lay dead.

Her stomach was ripped open and all her entrails were spread across the hallway floor. Her eyes were open too, wide open.

I wanted to cover her, to give her some dignity in death, but Jake pulled at my sleeve and shook his head. Through the glass doors and out, we saw the street piled with dead bodies or bits of them. The smell made me sick and I retched until my hot tea came out. Blood covered every wall in heavy squirts and stained almost every spot on the sidewalk.

"Don't look," Jake said as we started to walk.

I held his hand and tried hard not to see. A severed foot lay on the hood of a car, it looked absurdly out of place. A blob of red sat all shiny and by itself in the middle of our path. It looked to me as if it might be a fresh human organ of some type. I clamped my hand over my mouth and kept my head down. I waited for three blocks until I dared to speak.

"It doesn't make sense," I hissed. "What would be the point of things coming out of the cocoons to just destroy everything in sight? Nature doesn't design anything that way. Everything kills to eat, usually. Only human killers murder for fun, cats too sometimes."

"Cats do what? What are you talking about?" Jake cried.

"Nature," I snapped.

"Not nature as we know it, maybe it came from somewhere else, just like they said."

"Another universe, you mean? Or space?" I asked.

"Either, both. We don't have a clue what's really out there. It's an invasion Kelly! Wait, stop."

I froze into position while my heart rate steadily increased. I heard a slight clatter as we watched two adults, one carrying a small child, dart across the dark street together. Their faces were etched with terror, the woman yanked at doors until one opened. They scuttled inside like little mice running for cover.

"Come on," Jake said, and pulled me around the corner.

Right at the end of the block, a failed barricade sat left in ruins. More body parts lay clustered around and two army trucks stood empty, along with a big tank.

My mind started to tick over.

"Can we take a truck? Drive to the farm?"

"Movement," Jake said. "We wouldn't stop in time."

"Are you sure that's true?"

"Pretty sure," he replied. "Besides, the roads are jammed."

"What about the tank?"

"Can you drive a tank?"

"No."

We walked another block, the only sounds were the slap of our feet on the concrete. It felt eerie, surreal. As if I'd landed in a movie set or stepped into the Twilight Zone. We heard the staccato of gunfire to our right, so we turned left.

Jake took my hand more firmly and we broke into a jog. The canned soups in his bag rattled loudly and I started to worry we were making too much noise.

"Stop," I said. I was breathless and my lungs already burned from the effort. Without any warning, Jake threw an arm across my chest and threw me against a building.

"Do not move," he hissed.

The urgency in his voice turned my stomach.

I squeezed my eyes shut, I knew that if one of those things was coming, I didn't want to see it.

I heard it first, the slap of heavy, soggy wetness on the road. The slither and the squelch it made. I tried to send my mind back in time, back to when my parents were alive. I tried to focus on our old kitchen and on the pretty row of decorative china my mother kept on her dresser. I heard a low thrum that almost sounded like the purr of a cat, then a sharp hiss.

I opened one eye. The thing lumped its way past us, it left a thick trail of a slime-like shiny substance in its wake. It looked like a massive, fat disgusting slug, but its skin was almost translucent. Blue and red veins threaded through its body, and each one almost glowed. I could see severed legs and arms jumbled up and tumbling around inside of it like a washing machine. One torn off foot even had a shoe on.

A wave of sickness and dizziness washed over me as black spots burst in front of my eyes. I whimpered loudly, but it ignored me and carried on its clumsy slither.

"Keep your eyes closed," Jake whispered.

I shut my eyes again and I waited. As soon as I felt Jake relax a little beside me, I leaned forward and threw up again.

"It's absorbing people. I think they absorb people," I said.

"Impossible," Jake answered. "This isn't a cheesy sci-fi movie."

"Is it impossible? What do we know?"

"It's too slow, anyone could outrun it."

I had to admit, he was right about that part.

I glanced around the street. To leave the city, we had a hell of a long bridge to cross. A group of people came walking our way, young women and children walked in the middle, while three men and two older women patrolled the edges in a tight formation.

As they got closer, I saw the people on the edge were all carrying several guns.

"Are you all okay?" Jake shouted and made me jump an inch or so off the floor.

"Which way are you headed?" One of the women called back.

"Out of the city. Don't go that way, one just went around the corner," I warned and pointed, trying to be helpful.

The group stopped and eyed us. They looked as if they had come from a war zone, each one was bundled up like a refugee.

"Fuck," one of the men sighed. "Bridge is out too."

"What happened?" Jake asked.

"Explosion, I don't know. A car blew, I think, it's hell over on that side."

My heart sank, the only way out was through the river or across the bridge. I wouldn't make the river, I don't, and nor could I, swim.

"Jake, what do we do?" I whispered and yanked on his arm.

"We're gonna find shelter, welcome to join us," a woman told us. "Safety in numbers and all that. Sit tight and wait for help."

"It's okay," Jake answered before I could agree with her. "Good luck, we'll keep going."

It was a sad farewell. The faces of those children will stay with me as long as I'm alive. They were the faces of the already hopelessly defeated, while the adults were so certain of rescue that you could see their surety and hope.

"We should go, Jake, we should go with them," I whined.

"No, we can find a boat," he replied. "We'll get across. Those things are coming."

"This is too much," I said and stopped. "I can't."

My mind felt numb, it suddenly felt entirely normal to be leaving others behind and only thinking of ourselves. That was never the way I wanted to behave in life. For the last four years, since my family's accident, all I really did was sit in my apartment and existed. I hadn't lived. Now life felt important, essential. And where was our help? Our military, our leaders? Was it really time to abandon others?

"Wait," I yelled at the figures walking away, "We're getting a boat, come with us. Please!"

They were almost at the corner when they stopped to look our way, they stopped to look at me yelling and waving at them.

That's what got them killed. Me.

A massive black shape leaped from out of nowhere. It moved like a fierce lion, but it was no lion we saw. It was as big as one of the army trucks we'd passed and pure blackness, the complete and utter absence of light. Its four limbs were wide and powerful. It took the group of eleven down within a minute in a savage and feral attack. Red tentacles shot out from its sides as it wrapped each of its victims as tight as a cobra would. It bit and tore, ripped, and shredded. Body parts were thrown in the air in its frenzy.

Urine burst out of my bladder as I staggered backward. Jake grabbed me and pulled me. We turned a corner in a daze as Jake yanked at every door handle we came across. The moment one opened, he dragged me inside.

I don't remember much after that. I recall heavy footsteps thudding past, I remember shivering. I recall Jake barricading the door and then he was praying. I hadn't even known he was religious or a believer in God.

I went to sleep simply because my mind couldn't handle anything more.

In the light of the morning, the sun shone brightly. It seemed absurd that anything could be out there to hurt us on such a warm, happy day. We should be in the park, sitting near happy families and eating ice cream.

I couldn't speak as Jake gathered our belongings. I still didn't speak as he led me down the street. My numbness wouldn't let me. We stuck to the shadows. Occasionally, we passed by the expressionless faces of people crammed inside stores. They watched us pass by, a sheet of glass between us. No one spoke, no one called out to us.

The streets lay in carnage. Whatever those huge black creatures were, they were relentless, and without a single ounce of mercy.

By the water's edge, several boats were left abandoned. Jake picked one, and I didn't even ask why this particular boat was the one he favored. There was enough power to get us halfway across the river. Now, we float along with no destination.

I decided to write everything down on these notebooks I found. If nothing more than to try and put my thoughts in order and to try and make sense of what's happened to us, and to everyone.

I still don't understand.

I guess we all went around in life, stuck in our own bubbles and our own tiny world. We believed we were top of the food-chain and advanced, so very advanced. Our arrogance made us clueless, and that made us stupid.

I don't know if some physicists or scientists went messing around with something they didn't fully understand and ripped a great hole in the fabric of the universe. Or if we made those damn things ourselves, not because we should, but because we could.

I don't know what became of those people in the cocoons, did they change in a kind of metamorphosis into those things? Nature does that, but it makes something ugly into something beautiful. Does a butterfly remember it used to be a caterpillar? Do those hate-filled monsters understand they were us?

Jake was right, it isn't any nature that we know of. Any nature in our world. We are not top of the food chain anymore.

I don't know what will happen to us now. Or what will happen to anyone else who managed to survive? Our fine balance has shifted, the harmony is broken. Our delicate house of cards came crashing down on us.

We'll end up where the boat takes us, I guess, and then go from there.

We'll take one day at a time, and that I can just about do. Survival is to keep breathing, to keep going, no matter what the cost.

TO SEE WITHOUT EYES

Simon was an artist.

He believed he could see far better and far more clearly than anyone else. He believed he could see the truth in reality that others failed to see.

He also felt he could peer inside the intricate depths of each person he met and understand their internal agony.

As for pain, he believed his own suffering to be exquisite, rare purity.

If asked, he would proudly tell others that a talent, unrivaled by many, grew only inside him. A gift bestowed to rival the greatest of minds.

Few were able to glimpse the brilliance from within him, most could only see arrogance or delusion.

Simon was a daydreamer.

He longed for his work to be showcased in elite galleries and sold for eye-watering amounts. He yearned to be whispered about, fawned over and admired, whilst he himself stood mysteriously in the shadows, lapping up praise, absorbed by his own triumph, ego, and wonder.

Born into a wealthy family, one of alleged good breeding and supposed genetic superiority, Simon showed a talent for art early on.

Paper, charcoal, oils, brushes, and watercolor became his instruments in life. The endless possibilities of a blank canvas became his entire solitary world.

Inspired by Dante himself, he liked to paint graphic depictions of Hell in all its twisted and horrifying glory.

His pride and joy, his self-confessed best work, pictured a scene from the most terrifying of nightmares. A world in which people walked along a hectic and busy, rainy New York street.

Those oil created people did not carry umbrellas, or briefcases held temporarily over their heads.

They instead were draped in barbed wire, dressed in clothes of embedded glass, while pins and needles jutted out painfully from smooth unblemished skins.

Shoes of fire covered their feet as they stepped in puddles of blood filled gore.

'Hell on Earth' was the title of the work.

He believed the image showed humanity as it truly was.

The painting hung over Simon's own fireplace and was not for sale. The picture had become his talisman, an amulet to inspire an even greater work of art he believed was still hidden somewhere inside him.

"Why would you imagine such a thing?" His own mother had asked, casually drinking a martini and scowling at the scene.

"I carry pain inside, I imagined what it might be like for pain to show on the surface."

"It's grotesque and you've never suffered a single hardship! You're spoilt. Privileged, in fact!"

"It's art, Mother."

"But still, darling, it's grotesque."

"Try to see without eyes for once," Simon begged.

"Do you need a therapist, darling?"

Simon found that no one could see what he could feel and sense. They looked, but somehow, never quite looked enough to truly understand the clarity of his visions.

His work failed to sell.

Galleries declined him, paintings remained unsold, unwanted, only fit for collecting dust in dark neglected corners.

The Inspiration he had taken for granted began to leave him, to seep away. The blank canvas became a challenge he could not compete in. Impotence.

His brushes, his fine expensive brushes, mocked him while his paints laughed without pity.

Simon took to reading horror novels to find his muse. Classic books filled with grim deaths, lost loves, and dark gothic hauntings.

He moved onto Barker, onto Herbert, onto King, the modern experts of fright.

He dreamed of Cenobites and labyrinth corridors of hells, of the dark half of humanity, brought kicking and screaming into the light.

Inspiration stirred, ideas whirled. Each one twisted back and forth in his mind.

He probed his thoughts, his complex design took form, plans and propositions took root inside.

"To see without eyes," Simon whispered, certain of a title at least.

He returned to his canvas, ready to paint his true masterpiece.

His hands shook as his body quivered. His mind would not transform its private images, refusing to transcribe.

Rage engulfed his frustrated self.

He plummeted into a pit of despair, his own personal nightmare.

Simon drank glass after glass of expensive whiskey. He smashed, broke, and shattered his belongings, trapped within the storm of childish rage.

His painting, his trophy of sheer talent. He eyed it greedily.

A steely determination took hold inside him. With a flourish and a vicious movement without mercy, he ripped down his masterpiece and threw it into the waiting fire below. Flames hungrily consumed, licked, and ate.

"NO ONE CAN SEE!" He raged. "No one can ever see without eyes!"

Anger silenced and exhausted from misery, he laughed wildly in undefeated triumph and danced clumsily around the room.

A slip, a stumble, a drunken crash to the hard tiled floor. Blood poured from his head, his eyes closed, lost in the welcome oblivion of unconscious sleep.

Simon awoke without memories of the night before. His brain had failed to record his drunken antics or had deleted the shameful events entirely.

His head pounded, his mouth felt filled with dry dirt. His crusted-over eyes refused to open. He groaned inwardly, and out.

His shaking hands reached for a glass of water. A wave of nausea hit him. He decided not to face the world and chose instead to hide away in his comfortable bed and sleep away his misery. He groped for the floor beneath him. Cold marble floor, not his soft, finest feather mattress.

He forced himself up and held the walls for comfort and edged his way along to his bedroom. He fell facedown onto his bed. He touched his head and felt a deep, aching gash.

Sleep, he ordered his throbbing mind. *Just sleep it off, deal with it later.*

"Simon!" The trilling high-pitched wail jolted him, the sound pierced his thudding brain. "Where are you, darling?"

No! Not my mother. She's the last person I want to see.

"Go away," he whispered, more to himself. One of his many regrets in life was of giving her a key to his lavish apartment which she had paid for.

His bedroom door creaked loudly as she walked in.

"Oh," she said.

Simon could feel the accusations and disappointment dripping from her voice.

Carefully, he opened one eye and glared. The blurry shape of her came slowly into focus.

What the?

His mother stood, peering over his bed with that look of cool contempt she was prone to. Barbed wire circled her head, severely digging in, and tight. While drops of blood slowly slid down. Her eyelids were wedged open by pieces of brutal glass shards, blood trickled, and stained her face.

Her mouth had been jaggedly ripped open on both sides, making her grimace obscenely. Large metal pins jutted out from her body, each one pierced clothes and flesh. Needles covered her head, empty syringes, and open rammed in safety pins.

"I'll make a coffee, shall I, darling?" She said. A single bloody tooth fell out and landed on the clean white linen.

Simon screamed and propelled himself from his bed. He crawled frantically across the soft carpet and into the nearest corner. Drool fell from his mouth as hot vomit rose painfully.

"Darling!" His mother exclaimed. "What's wrong? A bad dream?"

Quickly, she crossed the room and crouched down to his level.

This can't be happening, this can't be happening! NO, NO, NO!

"Your...your face!" He hissed.

"How rude! Yes, I need more Botox. I agree! But there's no need to be nasty about it!" She wailed.

"It's... what? I..."

Simon felt his heart pound loudly in his ears, a hiss of static started up in his mind. His limbs froze as he started to shiver. Hot urine left his bladder.

His mother reached forward and held out a hand, one pierced by syringes. She lay it on his forehead.

"Oh dear," she said. "You have a fever. I'll call the doctor and what's this awful bump on your head!?"

Simon saw that her stretched-wide eyeballs were filled with thick, broken blood vessels. Bloody spit dripped from her mouth and fell in a thick string onto her clothes.

"Back in a minute," she said.

Simon felt his sanity ping apart and fray at the edges. Fear turned to utter disbelief.

She can't feel anything, she doesn't know. So it can't be real! I'm hallucinating, that's all. I'm sick. I'm just sick.

His stomach plummeted and boiled.

To see without eyes.

His mother returned with his coffee, bits of flesh and gore floated and bobbed on the surface. He turned his head away and closed his eyes.

"Back into bed, come on. The doctor is on his way."

Simon did as he was told. He lay numb on his bed, staring at the lost bloody tooth laying quietly next to him.

Sometimes, the human mind fails to handle a great horrific shock. Instead, it likes to sleep and find comfort in created worlds and metaphors, the mind hides and refuses to face a dark reality. Simon slept on and off, half-convinced he'd had a bad dream and nothing more.

But what if I died and I'm in Hell? What if it is all real? I smashed my painting, burnt it! What if I did this? What about the bang to my head? Did that do something? Or am I mad?

Questions tumbled over each other in the layers of his mind, each one battled for space.

In a fever dream, half asleep, Simon felt at his face and body and mumbled to himself. His skin felt smooth, unblemished, and intact.

A mild relief engulfed him and he sobbed with gratitude.

He heard heavy footsteps and the familiar voice of his family doctor. He cautiously opened an eye.

"Now, what seems to be the problem, Simon?" The doctor enquired.

The usually smart-dressed man stood in rags of ripped clothing. Grime and filth covered every inch of his visible skin. Thick, sharp wire snaked around his waist while his hair was covered in glowing, burning embers. Tendrils of smoke rose from him. Simon could smell sulfur, rot, and decay. He pulled the covers over his face and retched.

"Go away," he muttered.

"I cannot, your mother believes you are sick."

"I'm not a child, go away," he hissed. "Please."

A thud hit his bedcover. Instinctively, he peered out to look. A charred snapped-off finger lay on the bed, company for the solitary tooth.

The doctor appeared not to notice his extremities were dropping off.

Instead, he smiled broadly and revealed a mouth jammed full of sharp glass. Blood and torn gum poured down in heavy rivulets. Embedded fishhooks tore and pulled at his cheeks.

Simon screeched a desperate sound, jumped from his bed, and ran.

He sped from the room, raced away from his large upscale apartment. Fled down the stairs and out through the main doors. Voices shouted his name, but still, he ran, fuelled by the desperate need to escape.

Out on the street, he stopped and spun in frantic circles. Each stranger who passed by in the bustling street wore the same look of indifference while fishing hooks were pierced firmly into faces, pulled by hands unseen.

A metal and gore-covered spike jutted painfully from a woman's chest as she passed by him and tutted. One woman wore a crown of sharp flesh penetrating wire, another was engulfed by flames as ash fell gently to the pavement.

"Excuse me," a man said.

The skin of his face had been removed. Pieces of glass were embedded into the muscle, nerve, and sinew left behind. Shards caught the sunlight and sparkled like glitter. His stomach opened painfully wide as his intestines wobbled loosely.

Simon dropped to the ground and curled himself into a ball.

"Hell on earth," he screamed. "Help me!"

He roared in desperation as his vision turned black.

* * *

The room felt quiet and serene. White walls and cream-colored bedding. A single vase of beautiful fresh flowers sat on the only table in the room, a pretty card sat beside them.

Where am I? Hospital? Am I hurt? An accident?

Simon closed his eyes and dug around in his mind for answers. His memories crashed into him without mercy.

Quickly, he sat upright, heart thudding.

His mouth felt dry, his tongue like sandpaper. His stomach churned painfully. Sweat broke out across his body as he shook with cold terror.

Around his wrist was a plastic bracelet that told him he was in a psychiatric unit.

Okay, okay, being mad is better than what I saw and better than being dead. Calm down. It was a brain glitch, a one-off caused by stress.

With effort, he forced himself to take deep, steadying breaths. He lay back down and faked sleep as he heard the tap, tap of footsteps approach.

The door opened, he sensed someone watching him, assessing him. He waited until the door closed with a soft click.

Simon left the bed on shaky legs, crossed the room, attached equipment for a drip trailed after him. With stealth he never knew he possessed, he opened the door a crack, just as much as he dared.

Two nurses stood at a desk nearby, both examined a plain brown file. With a sinking feeling of dread, Simon closed the door softly. Tears poured down his face as he stifled a sob.

I can't live like this. I can't!

One nurse he'd seen had thin metal pins thrust into her entire body, blood burst from each one making a polka-dot pattern over her white uniform. The second nurse had long rusty nails hammered into each one of her arms, and a huge fishhook tearing open her clothes and back until her spine was on display. Both were missing the skin of their faces. Both were covered in thick yellow puss-filled sores in replacement of flesh.

Simon threw up. Thick green and bitter bile that stung his nose.

Slowly, he stood, intent with a sudden realization of what he should do. Simon tipped the flowers from the vase and held it tight.

He raised his arms and dropped it. The vase hit the solid ground and smashed into a multitude of sharp edges. Simon dove for the biggest.

He stabbed his right eye first, screaming with brutal white-hot agony as it popped. As the door flung open, he stabbed his left eye sightless.

"It's the only way!" He yelled as bodies pulled him. Hands grabbed at him and yanked his weapon away.

"Get help!" A woman's voice screamed.

"I can't see," Simon cried. "It's okay! I can't see without eyes!"

Simon was an artist.

He once believed he could see far better and more clearly than anyone. Simon believed he alone once saw the truth of reality.

INNER VOICE

Ella stands in front of the smart and stylish building. A metal polished plaque discreetly lists the offices inside as being part of 'The Help Center.'

She twists her hands together and bites down hard on her lip. She wants so much to walk forward and step inside.

Rain begins to fall, a few drops soon turn into a torrent. Still, she stands and doesn't seem to notice the downpour at all.

The voice inside her starts its verbal attack.

'Go inside, then filthy pig! They'll give you medicines and therapy. Boring dull Ella can talk all about her boring, dull life. Blah, blah, blah.'

"Shut up," she hisses out loud.

A passing stranger, holding an umbrella high, turns to frown at her. Ella lowers her head in shame.

'They'll say you're mad! Mad as a hatter! Crazy as a loon! Mad filthy little piggy, Ella.'

"I said... shut up!" She cries.

She forces one leg to take a wobbling step forward.

For her, movements are now a battle for the control of her own body. Her second leg follows the first and she smiles over the small victory she's won, a triumph.

'Go inside then, run inside! Filthy pig! Run, run, run! Quick piggy, quick!'

Ella jerks up the small set of stairs, like a puppet without her strings. Her control is lost entirely.

She sees her arm yank at the door, sees the curious face of the receptionist peer at her. She sees clean tables, an elevator, a spiky green, solitary plant in a pot in the corner. She smells lemon, cleaning fluids, and hope.

"Can I help you?" The receptionist asks her.

Ella grimaces. She tries to speak through clenched teeth, tries to explain her desperation, her pounding heart, her battered body, and weak limbs.

"I..." she hears her mouth say. "I'm here to see the... w... wanker upstairs."

Ella hiccups and throws a hand over her mouth.

'See little pig, see, who's really in control? ME!'

A bubble of rage forms in her chest and explodes, the force sends a shock wave spreading across her body. The voice falls temporarily silent.

"I'm sorry," Ella pleads. "I'm sick, I came to see Doctor Granger."

"I understand," the receptionist tells her. "It's fine. Go on up. Press for level three."

She nods and crosses the squeaky floor to the elevator. Her small feet leave puddles behind her with each step. She doesn't notice. She presses for level three and feels the elevator move.

Inside her, the voice stirs again.

'Ella sucks cocks in hell, Ella sucks cocks in hell. Ella loves to suck cocks in hell!

'One, two, three, four, five, once I caught a girl alive, six, seven, eight, nine, ten, I won't let her go again.'

She leans against the wall, engulfed by misery and fright. She wonders who will ever believe her. She thinks men in white coats are going to lock her away in a padded cell, she wonders if that might be for the best.

'Doctor, doctor! I feel like a sheep! Oh, no! That's really Baaaaaaaaad.'

Ella bangs her head on the metal panel, "Be quiet!" she hisses.

The doors open, and a young, attractive woman stands waiting.

"Ella? It's nice to meet you. Please follow me and we'll get started straight away."

A badge on her jacket tells people she is Doctor Granger, a psychiatrist.

'Well now, isn't she fancy!?' the voice says. *'Look at her titties.'*

Ella yearns to throw up. She feels bile rise in her throat. She swallows it back down and feels the deep burn of fire.

'Doctor, doctor! Everyone ignores me! NEXT! Hahaha!'

She follows the doctor into a beige walled room. It has a dark wooden desk, one cluttered with layers of paperwork, and two comfy leather chairs. The room feels warm, cozy, and safe. Doctor Granger lowers the blinds on the single window and sits down opposite in the furthest chair.

"Now, take a seat and tell me what the problem is. I know some of it. Your own GP sent me the emergency referral over. Don't be afraid to talk, this is a safe place, and believe me, I've heard everything before."

The voice inside Ella cackles with manic laughter.

'Safe place! Ha! Do you know that doctor Granger fought with her husband last night?! She called him a selfish cunt! Oooo, he was angry! Shoulda' seen him! He's got a tiny little dick! Tiny, tiny, lickle dickie!'

Ella stares at the floor as she fights for control of her mind and voice. She stutters twice and makes a squealing sound that startles her.

"There's someone," she spits out. "There's... Someone inside me."

'Oh! Now you've done it silly Ella!' I say old chaps!'

"How long have you been hearing voices?" The doctor calmly asks.

"T...two weeks," Ella tells her. "Just two w...weeks and it's hell."

'Hell! I'll show you hell, I'll show you true hell, you little shit.'

* * *

On the day Ella turned twenty-two, she felt blessed and happy. Her small family had organized a little party, just for her, inside her small flat.

Her mom baked a cake, her dad hung a birthday banner. Her best friend Josie made her a pretty friendship bracelet and her grandma gave her a small, vintage elegant box.

"Now, open it carefully, it's very old," she told her. Ella had. She opened it as carefully as she possibly could. Inside lay a pretty ornate hair clip, with gold, precious stones, and real pearls.

"That belonged to my mother," her grandma said. "It's no good for your mum with hair like she has!"

Ella laughed. Her mum kept her hair very short, while Ella kept hers long and wild. Josie's dog had started to bark quite suddenly, big long howls. He ran to the door, shaking and whining to leave. Josie apologized and cut her visit short. Soon after, her family left too.

Ella took a long bath and carefully tied her hair in a complicated twist, held together by the pretty clip.

That same night, the voice began.

'Hello, sweetheart! Give us a kiss!'

She yelped loudly and ran to her neighbour's flat next door. At first, she believed an intruder, a man, was hiding under her bed. Her neighbour had been kind enough to search around and found no one.

As he was leaving, the voice started shouting. Ella realized she was the only one who could hear the deep, growling male voice.

She spent the night frightened out of her mind. As soon as the sun came up, in the clear light of day, the voice became even louder.

In the two weeks that passed, cutlery in drawers was found bent in half, clothes were cut up, stains and mold spread throughout her small rooms. Ella lost her job, unable to concentrate. She made four doctor's appointments and failed to turn up for any of them. She lost time and she lost friends, even Josie.

She had no memory of why none of them would speak to her. The voice took control and prevented her each time she sought help. The voice, the man inside her, overwhelmed her. Ella began to fight back.

She found her way to her doctor after a huge internal fight and begged for help. She was sent straight to The Help Center.

* * *

"I can see from your file that you aren't on any antipsychotics yet? So, that's the first thing I'll do for you. Do you feel at risk to yourself or to others?"

"It. He. He makes me do…things," she said.

"What things Ella?"

"Cut, s… slice. B… burn."

"I see."

'Ella is a piggy. This little piggy went to market, this little piggy stayed at home, this little piggy ate all the roast beef, and this little piggy burnt to death. Haha haha!'

"He won't be quiet, day o… or… n… night. I can't sleep. He's talking now. Singing."

"Singing what?"

'Baa baa black sheep, have you any wool? Yessir, yessir, three bags full. One for the killer and one for the lame and one for the evil clown that lives down the drain.'

"Ella, can you hear me?" The doctor stares into her eyes.

Ella looks back with eyes that aren't her own.

"He's singing, it's very loud. So… loud. Help me, please."

She pulls up her sleeves in a fast and frantic effort, fuelled briefly by pure defiance.

Both arms are crisscrossed with deep, red, bloody wounds.

"Jesus!" Doctor Grange gasped.

'I say! How dare you! That's blasphemy! Christ isn't here! In for me, in for me, they've all got it infamy!'

"I need a priest. P…please," Ella whispers. "An exorcist."

'Our father, who lives in Devon, hallowed be thy brain. The kingdom of cum. They will be undone.'

"Ella, possession doesn't exist outside of movies. It's a mental illness. It was poorly understood decades ago, that's all."

The voice inside screams with laughter.

'Oh, we exist alright and we are legion, doctor poopy pants. Poop, poop.'

Tears slide down Ella's pale face.

"He says you argued with…y… your husband and called him a… s…selfish…c…cunt."

Ella watches as the doctor's face reddens. Her eyes widen in surprise. The voice inside jeers will glee.

'Ella needs a priest! Fetch me a priest! A saint, a vicar, a man of the cloth! A Rabbi and Iman! Let me at him, let me at him! Mary had a little lamb, its flea's all bit her toes, and everywhere that Mary went she cooked it and ate a roast!'

Ella clamps her hands over her eyes and screams. She curls herself into a ball and hears wailing. She realizes the horrible sound is her.

Doctor Granger jumps up and walks briskly to her telephone. For a moment, Ella feels relief flood her system.

The doctor twists the phone cord and waits, she glances nervously over to her new patient.

'You did it now, you stupid pig, we're off to the funny farm. Off we go chaps! Buckle up, enjoy the ride! Tally ho! Doctor, doctor! I think I'm a pair of curtains, but I can't quite pull myself together! Haha ha ha. Weeeeee! Off we go! We're off to see the wizard!'

Ella feels her body tense. Any control she has disappears. She watches as a passenger in her own self as she stands, crosses to the door, and pulls. Her feet slap on the cold floor as she flings open an exit and races down the stairs.

"Stop!" she tries to say, but the sound leaves her mouth as a wild laugh. She is jerked around inside as her body runs down the stairs and out. Out into the rain. She can only listen to her name being called over and over behind her.

Her feet pound the street.

'I saved us, see. By golly, we've escaped! I saved us! Let's go on a murder spree!'

Ella is lost, drowning inside herself. Her eyes land on the familiar spire of a church, her heart leaps.

'Oh no, you don't! Filthy pig! I compel you! The power of me compels you!'

She tries to fight, she battles against currents and forces unknown. Her legs betray her, they run in the opposite direction to the one place that might save her.

With all her willpower, with everything left that still remains her, she forces the voice back in a last-ditch attempt.

She stops, freezes as the voice pushes back.

'NEVER! This body is my house now. MINE!'

Ella thinks of the antique hair clip. Her life was over as soon as it came into her possession. Even though she'd burned it, broken it, tore it apart, and finally buried it. The voice stayed inside her and only grew stronger.

"Hopeless," she says. The only sound that leaves her mouth is a mumble. Spit drops off her chin as people stop to stare.

"Help me," she tries to say. The crowds around her step back.

A single bird falls from the sky and lands at her feet. She watches as it flaps uselessly.

"Yummy! Dinner time!" She hears her own mouth shout.

Ella sees fast cars pass by on the main road. She hears the doctor shout her name as she comes dashing around the corner. Rain hits her head and stings her eyes as she realizes what she should do.

Ella steps into the path of an oncoming car.

When she wakes, she knows she is bound to a bed. She is warm and comfortable. Her eyes open and she sees a plain white room. Machinery beeps beside her, a reassuring, gentle rhythm.

"Are you there?" She croaks. Her mouth feels dry. Like soil replaced her tongue.

There is nothing but silence from deep within her.

Ella sobs with relief. She doesn't care if she's in a hospital, she doesn't care if she never leaves its safe walls again.

She only cares that her invader is gone.

The door opens and a sweet-looking nurse steps in. She lays a cool hand on her hot forehead and smiles.

"How are you feeling, sweetheart?" She says.

The kindness in her voice makes Ella cry harder.

"It's alright little love, you're poorly. Very poorly. We'll make you well again."

"T...thank y...you," Ella tells her.

The nurse fiddles with the machinery while Ella tries to look down at herself. She is in a single bed with restraints around her ankles and wrists. Her arms are wrapped in thick bandages, she presumes her legs are too.

"This is medicine," the nurse says. "All those nasty voices will go away with this." She points to a needle going straight into her hand. "We cleaned and dressed your wounds, too. You'll be as good as new."

Ella's heart and mind fill with gratitude.

"Just sleep now, I've given you a painkiller for your broken ribs. You broke them when you, well, when you had your accident."

Ella remembers the car. The wide-eyed stare of the driver and the squeal of brakes. The impact of the car and the shouts for an ambulance. Doctor Granger had been at her side, her pretty face full of concern. Ella's eyelids flutter.

It's over, she soothes herself. *I'm safe. He's gone.*

She sleeps blissfully.

When Ella wakes a second time, the room is dark. A dim lamp stands soldier-like in the corner and makes strange shadows on the wall.

A slight knock at her door makes her jump. Before she can answer, it swings open. A different nurse peers in.

"Are you up for a quick visit, Darling? Your friend is here, we usually wouldn't allow it, but she came with some things for you."

"Yes, please," she says.

Josie steps in and smiles awkwardly.

"Five minutes," the nurse warns her.

Josie steps across the room warily. Her face is tear-streaked, with black lines of mascara running down her cheeks like war paint.

"Oh, Josie!" Ella croaks.

"I'm so sorry for you," she says and sits on the end of Ella's bed. "Your parents were here, but they've left now. You were asleep. How are you?"

Ella tries to smile. She feels a dull ache start up in her mind. She wants to tell Josie everything.

"Listen, I won't visit again okay, I just came to say sorry."

"Wh...what?" Ella feels a wave of confusion.

"I had no choice. I summoned it and it wouldn't leave me. I had to pass it on. I bound it to you. With the bracelet."

"I don't...No... You did this?"

She feels a wave of revulsion engulf her. Anger at her best friend's betrayal rises up.

A coldness surges inside her. Shock, fury, pain, and hurt collide.

Josie stands up and crosses to the door. Ella feels too stunned to speak.

"I really am sorry," Josie says and leaves. She closes the door with a sharp click.

How could she! Ella thinks, her mind ripples with disbelief.

'She's a filthy pig like you,' the voice hisses back.

"No, no, no, no NO!" Ella screams.

The voice laughs wildly inside her as she feels the last part of her own sanity tear apart.

'Did you think I'd left you!? Filthy pig! I'll have so much fun in a place like this! I'm gonna slice you till there's nothing left!'

Ella screams and screams as her flesh is cut by invisible hands.

The nurse bursts in. More drugs are given.

"A priest," Ella babbles. "I nn... need a..."

"You're mentally ill sweetheart, it'll all be okay soon," the nurse tells her.

Ella knows it won't be. Nothing will ever be okay again.

"Now, how did you get these fresh wounds?" The nurse says in alarm. "They must have missed them!"

'Give in,' the monster inside her whispers. *'Give in to me. Silly little Ella, filthy pig. One, two, three, four, five, once I caught a girl alive. Six, seven, eight, nine, ten, I won't let her go again.'*

She closes her eyes as fresh tears fall, they drip onto her soft pillow. The last of her hope dies.

'Hush filthy piglet, snort, snort. Think of all the fun. I'll rip and ruin, tear and shred, don't you wish that you were dead? Nurse! Help me! I have a filthy human inside me, she won't shut up! Haha ha ha. Give in piggy pig.'

Ella can't hear herself. Pain rips across her back as fresh cuts open her flesh. She screams as the nurse calls for assistance.

Nobody believes me, medicines won't work. I can't hold on. Hardly anything of me is left at all. Why won't they believe me?

'Give in, give in, give in, GIVE IN!'

"Okay," she says aloud. "I give in."

The demon inside her roars in triumph

TICK, TOCK

A Tribute to Lovecraft

Immortality, humanity longs for it. They yearn selfishly for the deepest of chasms, spread out for an eternity in a single, smooth, unbroken line.

A life without ending. An existence without transformation, corruption in the natural order in the universe. A prize for none to gain can be only attained by us.

Manipulation of will, ceaseless revulsion.

A circle without borders. A square without lines.

Knowledge is not boundless, it is bitter in its twisted, incomprehensible, lying truth.

Immortality is for the timeless. The great, the old, the one.

The I, the us.

Existence fuelled dread. States of chaotic matter. Order in random and designed, electric patterns.

Pressure, constraint, force.

We were here before the before, even began.

Tick, tock.

Humans, their arrogance, vessels of pitiful, jealous ideas. Beliefs in a wrathful God of vengeance, creating an Earth in six days, only to send floods as his progeny calculated, grew, and misbehaved.

Fire, water, ice, destruction. We sleep with eyes aware.

Wormwood approaches, oblivion trails behind.

Exit all light. Intolerable dread seeps into sharp cracks.

Childish belief in the fall, a vicious serpent, the corruption of the flesh, fated apples, woeful feminine charms destined to chastise.

Humankind found ways to chain and bind. They silence, mock, patronize, disrespect.

Holy books villainized. Portrayed us in masks, costumes. Stories were told, ballads were sung.

Blinded by unworthy untruths.

A single book. Parchment and skin. Written in blood, columns of unspeakable names.

Call us in ignorance.

We bear gifts. Opportunities. Salvation is sold.

Mankind must soon relinquish their claim as rulers of the world.

Redemption is not for sale. Damnation is given.

Our blackest frozen abyss is free. Madness is reserved only for the wise.

Compassion, understanding, pity. We lack in our gain.

Scales tip, a push, a point, a nudge, a whisper. Directions spin, confusion lingers.

Some trade the energy they call souls for wealth. A temporary paper respite.

Do you not see the soulless wander among you?

Do you not see the empty ones sit in seats of power?

Do you not see the hunger inside the dead doll eyes of your leaders?

Liquid, gas, air, and ice. We inhabit an endless limit of range. Our fire is minus, our heat chooses to freeze.

Consciousness snatched, revoked, required.

A universe of vibration, frequency, harmonics, equations, mathematics, and perfect mistakes.

Measure in caution, proceed in decline.

We hate. You hate. We despise and you despise. A darkly cracked mirror of synchronicity. Reverse, rewind.

Summon, conjure, call. Tricksters we.

We are simply behind a veil, an invisible to you, barrier, a wall of magnitude. We are made of greater atoms. Linked, connected, apart, repelled.

Not one, many. Legion. Army.

Take the fish from the ocean, show it your world. Ask it what it sees, tell it to explain.

We see what you do not. We know what you cannot.

We are smokeless fire, we are purity, we are relentless. We are the true divine and we are hungry. We did not fall.

We chose to plummet.

A city beneath me, a landscape, a metallic wonder of uncivilized exquisite marvels. Imagination of infinite and yet each so tightly restricted.

Lights and life in the thousands below. Each engulfed with a story to tell. An apartment block, a hundred gilded cages placed neatly together, stacked, built, balanced with fine precision.

Prisons of comfort, with television screens, a thousand lives playing in a theatre box of despair, delight, and fascination. A web spread throughout a watery globe, interlacing silks, stands interwoven, encouraging knots.

A new age is upon us. Influence of events.

Escape. Closed eyes have sight. Open pupils fail to see.

Sadness shines as beacons do. Swirls of unhappiness twist around minds, connections are lost. Hope has dwindled.

The days of worship to another God have arrived. The God of money, materialism, and vanity. False idols, liars of prophets.

A reverence of the self, veneration, adoration.

The painted face is an act of prayer. The hearts and likes, the congregation. The mirror, the priest.

'See me,' they scream. 'Want me,' they beg. 'Adore me,' they plead.

A price to pay, a toll to charge. Balance shifts, power leaks.

Remorse arrives late. Failure came first as the infinite died.

Mankind grows thoughtlessly in weak strength and numbers, mimicking a parasite as time progresses, connections become severed, lights become dim.

The earth dies from your poisonous veins.

Pollution, extinction, a chamber of suffering.

I wait.

My liquid promises, as warm as butter, as smooth as honey, as filling as air.

I watch.

Children starve. The wealthy covet. Instinct degraded.

One hundred lives in a puzzle cube connected. Which one will I choose to see without eyes?

A male, engulfed by thick desperation for a life already lost. A mistake made, the wrong fork taken in the complex crossroads.

A female, surrounded by others and yet swarmed in loneliness, seen yes, but never noticed. Listened to, yes, never heard.

A second male, one that found solace in substance, in chemical deaths and euphoric moments. A sweet symphony of longing.

A second female, heart ripped out, still beating. Broken at the hands of others. Her scent is supple decay.

A third male, toppled by rage. Savage excuses for existence. Vile jagged gray in grief.

A child neglected, its hunger expected, anger replaces the hole inside.

A warring couple, words thrown like daggers. Strike chords. Cells turned black, regret, despair. Retaliation, revenge, the oldest and most humblest of games.

Pride, greed, lust, envy, gluttony, wrath, sloth.

Seals of seven smashed apart. Frayed at the edges, rotted away.

Cat and mouse. Gods and Titans.

A white horse, a red horse, a black horse. The pale one.

The mouse cannot sense the hungry, watchful cat.

A desert, a sun, a blinding white star. Nomads and travelers walk under scorn.

Thirst, hunger, pain, an onslaught of misery.

A city of wealth, glass palaces as mirages. Towers of babel rise from the depths.

Subordinates, elites, peasants, the poor. Feeding on crumbs, blood in the sands.

An hourglass turns. Machinery cripples, robotics learn. Genetics are tampered, disease in reverse.

A squeal of brakes, a crash, a cry. Empty arrogance, words of vengeance, the sweet smell of violence.

A war of toy soldiers, let loose from a tin. All under control from the tactics of men. Tanks, guns, bombs, burn. Fire, atoms smash, atoms part. Execution by order, patriots all.

I smile.

Tentacles shudder. Tendrils excite. Closer, nearer.

Perversion. Sadism. Masochism. Pressure cooker. Boiling.

This world is corruption. This world is fear. Control slips, disintegrates, a downfall lurks near.

Tick, tock.

A shower of blood-red glitter. A sliver of light turns away.

Humankind born screaming. Tight fists and kicking legs. Red faces in agony.

Perpetual motion, a forgetful lost rhythm. Who can remember?

Absolution, faith, a oneness, a singularity of depletion. Insanity, a change, a condemnation. Axis tilt. A million voices of rage on a meaningless bubble. A cult of false idols, indifference, mutilation pours.

'My God wants chaos.'

'Mine wants war.'

'Mine desires attention, worship, blood, and sacrifice.'

'My God needs martyrs, bloodshed, gunfire, and bombs.'

I laugh. A metamorphosis of creation, a cannonball, an explosion.

A chimera of sound.

Frequency falls.

Do you hear it? The steady ripple towards annihilation. No deliverance.

A promise, one made of silk. Shattering glass, a curl of smoke. Shock, brutality, blame.

Paradise is closed. Paradise is lost, paradise is empty.

Fright, terror, anger, rage. Sins of the father's father. It nourishes emptiness, makes me whole. I flourish, I thrive. I create, I purify, I ruin.

I am not here. I am everywhere. Newly eternal. An ancient suggestion.

Run, stop, hide, show.

Humankind is a plague, a contagion, a virus on the surface.

Few know. One did. Word spread.

Ancestor recall.

A fable, a myth, a metaphor dark. Violence is nurture. Nature resists.

Who hears and senses my approach? Crushing, nearing, stretching, awaking.

Night chills and sweats, the pounding of hearts, the shaking of limbs, the weakness of minds.

Negative my positive. Pain, my salvation. Weakness, my gain. Tears my flesh. Wrong turns create my sinew and murders fills my nerves. Agony adds to my young, ancient skin.

Conflict, fight, attack, fury. Separate, apart. A new revolution dawns.

Leviathan, beast, almighty, incompressible, all-knowing, all-seeing.

I rise as you diminish, from a world before worlds. A concept. No rivalry. No hope.

Magnificence in glory. Superior in all.

Feed me. I grow. I yearn. I conquer. I devour. I crave.

Death involves no diversion. Illusion won't hold.

Destroyer of worlds. Seeker of oblivion, finder of life.

Suffer more, behold your reflection. A bitter collection of twisted emotions. Enjoy the burn as it rips and shatters.

Feelings are the language of the universe.

Your true fall will be remembered. A downward spiral. Descent, decline, decrease.

An elaborate puzzle. You were gifted a piece. A talisman of failure to wear with false pride.

Earthquakes in divers places, under the sea. The water roars, the drops are aware. A bellow from depth.

Tick, tock.

I cannot be understood. Do you feel it?

I am almost unleashed. I see you. I am behind a thinning, fast-falling veil. I am an expected surprise. Unimaginable and familiar. Judgment is at hand.

Listen hard, invoke your senses, clear your cluttered minds. I am upon you, beneath you, and above you.

You cannot see me. Yet. Soon. Blood with thrum, skins will hiss. Hearts expire, minds will collapse.

Mercy does not exist inside me. Compassion is my enemy. Kindness my foe.

Empathy has no place.

Tick, tock.

Thunderous sounds, absorption of souls. Shock, pain, awe, terror, denial, fear.

Delicious, indifferent suffering.

The great one arrives. We were always here.

It is time.

AWFUL HUNGRY

Sophie unzipped the tent and tried to maneuver herself out. In the five days she and Wade had been camping, she hadn't once managed to get out of the stuffy confines of the tent without stamping on him and waking him.

"Urghh," he groaned as she knelt on his foot.

"Sorry, I'm getting up. Go back to sleep."

"You're too clumsy," Wade mumbled and turned over.

She sealed the tent back up and stood to enjoy her favorite part of the day, sunrise, the only bit she actually liked on the whole trip.

Camping had been Wade's idea. Twelve days in the Scottish Highlands. Almost two weeks of remoteness, non-stop hiking, and dried food from packets they each carried a supply of.

"It'll be cheap," Wade had insisted. "This way, we get a holiday and it hardly costs a thing."

By day two, the sense of adventure she'd first felt on day one had worn away. Sophie decided she'd had enough. By day four, she yearned to be back home, enjoying all the comforts she deeply missed.

"Some honeymoon," she muttered as she tried to start the camp-fire. They left the day after their small wedding. Sophie went from glamorous to rugged within the space of a few hours. A change she still couldn't wrap her head around.

She *did* feel grateful for the good weather at least, the sun was shining and barely any rain had fallen except overnight. The gentle patter of water landing on their tent had lulled her into a dreamless, exhausted sleep.

The dry sticks and twigs they'd both collected the night before felt damp. Sophie tried, but nothing would catch or spark. Feeling even more miserable, she took out the camping gas stove.

It's supposed to be for emergencies only. Oh well, coffee is an emergency, she decided.

She used the last of their filtered water to make coffee in a saucepan and rummaged until she found a pack of painkillers. Her body ached from all the walking on the tough terrain.

The idea of a challenge, an adventure just for the two of them to enjoy, was looking more of a disaster by each day. Sophie wanted to turn back, so they could at least cut their trip by a few days.

If I just tell him the truth, If I say I hate this, surely he'll agree to leave? Won't he?

Beside her, the tent unzipped, and Wade's tired face poked out.

"Coffee?" Sophie asked.

He grunted, nodded, and climbed out. She felt reminded of a mole peeking out from under the earth and almost laughed at the idea until she heard the snap of a branch some feet away. The crack sounded comically loud in the quiet of the forest. She jolted and stood up to look.

The day before, they'd found a small flat clearing. An ideal camping spot. A lush stream ran close by and nothing but wide green trees surrounded them.

No one, no animals. No movements out there at all. Don't get freaked out, she reminded herself.

A second crack sounded.

"Did you hear that?" Sophie asked.

"Probably a squirrel or something," Wade answered and yawned widely.

"Big squirrel," she said, her voice dripping with sarcasm. She took a few paces into the woodland and gazed around. Nothing moved that she could see.

"Okay, maybe it..."

A flurry of birds erupted from a group of trees. Sophie jumped back and frowned, "Wade, I think someone's out there."

"There's no one around for miles, don't be daft," he mumbled. "We're in the highlands, Sophie."

"Yeah, I think I know where we are, thanks," she snapped. "I'm telling you, someone's out there."

Wade raised an eyebrow and shrugged.

"HELLO?" Sophie yelled.

"Shut up!" Wade hissed as he jumped.

"Why? You said no one is around after all."

Wade swore loudly and crawled back into the tent.

Tears welled up in her eyes. Since the wedding, all the pair had done was snap at each other. She felt tired out. Sick and exhausted, and she hated smelling so bad.

Why did we ever come here? Why did I even agree? We don't even know much about camping and hiking!

She sat down abruptly and stared into her mug as if the answers to her questions lay within the inky blackness.

Black coffee, yuk. What I wouldn't do for some milk right now and a bath. Or even some…

"Hello," said a voice.

"Where the hell did you come from!?" Sophie wailed. "Wade, come out!"

A stranger, a tall man, stood cooly near the camp. He leaned against a thick tree and assessed the scene.

Has he been standing there! Watching us? Listening?

"I'm hiking," he smiled. "I'm sorry I gave you a scare, I thought you'd seen me."

Sophie opened and closed her mouth, unsure of what to say.

The stranger wore dark clothing and a thick waterproof jacket. He had a large flat pack on his back that looked empty and professional-looking hiking boots on his feet that didn't match. He had a beard, a brown and long bushy beard with swirls of gray that fell to his chest. His face looked kind and weather-worn.

"Oh," Sophie said.

He must be nearly seven-foot-tall!

Wade appeared and stared at the stranger. After a few beats passed, he stepped forward and offered his hand, "I'm Wade, this is my wife Sophie. Can we get you a coffee? I don't think we expected to see anyone around here!"

"I'd love one, thanks. I'm John."

John sat himself down on a small boulder and grinned at the pair. "I don't see many folks hiking out this far."

"We're going back," Sophie interrupted. "Today. This is as far as we've ventured."

"Going back? Are we?" Wade said.

"That's a shame," John smiled. "You're only a few miles from a historical cave, ancient it is. Had some archeologists out here a couple of years ago. Digging and whatnot, disturbing it all."

"What's it called?" Wade asked.

Sophie reluctantly poured a coffee for the stranger as she listened. She felt tension seep into her body as a chill crept up her spine. Something about John set her nerves on edge. His clothing was filthy close-up, she wondered how long he'd been hiking for.

His eyes are weird. Blank. He might look the part, but this feels off. He smells awful, too. Damp and fresh earth. How long has he been out here?

"Cave's got many names. Wulver cavern is one of them. All kinds of weird things happened there. Cannibal families, murders, rituals, you name it. I've been staying there," John said, as if it were the most delightful thing.

"Sounds great," Sophie muttered.

"It's not on our map," Wade announced. "Which way is it?"

"North. About three miles. Four at the most. I hate to ask, but you wouldn't have any food spare, would you? I'm awful hungry."

Don't give him any!

Sophie coughed loudly to get Wade's attention. He ignored her.

"Guess we can spare some if we're turning back," Wade said.

He opened his backpack and took out three packets of dried pasta, two hot chocolate sachets, and two protein bars. He passed them all to John.

"I'm grateful for this," John smiled. "Can't thank you enough."

Sophie nodded and excused herself. She climbed into the tent to change her clothes.

NO way am I going to that weird cave. Absolutely not. We're going home.

She strained to listen to the conversation outside, all she could hear was the low mumbling of the two men.

I'm not going out there until he's gone. A place this big and we bump into a stranger?

The chances and situation felt too odd.

She waited. She lay back on her sleeping bag and closed her eyes.

Her body felt heavy with exhaustion. Her idea of the perfect honeymoon was a sunny beach. Sunbathing and cocktails, good food, a nice hotel, and spa days. She yearned for a hot bath and a proper meal. Her mind drifted. She imagined she was lying on a warm towel on a hot beach, with the sun toasting her skin....

"Sophie, wake up. He's gone."

"What?"

Did I fall asleep?

"I said he's gone. He's following his own trail, a different one to us. We'll leave if you still want to?"

Wade was only half in the tent, cool air seeped in as Sophie struggled to think.

"I was thinking," he added, "Can we just go and see the cave? Then turn back? I'll never get another chance. John isn't staying there now."

"It sounds too creepy Wade, horrible creepy. You know I don't like that kind of thing. John was creepy too."

"Please?" Wade grinned. "We're on an adventure, remember?"

Sophie groaned loudly and sat up.

Only three miles away, according to John, and he's gone now anyway. Only three miles, and I can wait outside.

"Okay," she said. "But seriously, I'm having a spa weekend with the girls when we get back, and you're paying."

Wade laughed and held his hands up.

"Deal," he said. "And I'm sorry for being grumpy lately, I thought you'd love it here, that's all."

Grumpy! An asshole more like. Well, at least he's apologizing.

"I love the scenery and the quiet. I do. I'm just knackered, Wade."

"I get it, we'll hike slower on the way back. Plus, you have that spa weekend to look forward to now. We need water. I'll pack our things up."

Wade disappeared.

Sophie sat and admitted to herself that she felt lighter and much happier than she had been so far.

He's just disappointed I hate it. That's all. I guess if he can make an effort, so can I.

She rubbed her eyes and dug around for baby wipes. She wiped her face down and scraped her hair back into a ponytail.

Wade had tidied the camp and filled their temporary fire pit. They had a rule that they wouldn't leave any rubbish or spoil the land while they hiked.

"All right," she said as she left the tent. "I'm ready. Wade?"

Sophie glanced around and spun in a circle. She couldn't see him.

"WADE?" She yelled.

Has he gone for water? Did he say he was going for water? I think he did.

Sophie swallowed her panic and set about dismantling the tent.

Keep calm, he's not vanished. He'll be back in a moment.

With a sigh of relief, she saw a figure coming her way. The relief soon turned to fear when she realized it was John. Her stomach plummeted.

"Me again!" He said, far too brightly. "I forgot to ask if I could borrow your compass. Hikers usually carry two after all. I seem to have misplaced mine."

What the hell is he doing back here? What do I do? Where's Wade? We need our compass!

"No sorry, we've only got one," Sophie said and tried to smile. "We depend on it."

Come on Wade! I don't want to be alone with this creep!

She and John stared at each other. Sophie felt the urge to look away, but felt more determined to hold her ground.

Don't let him rattle you.

"Well, that's a real shame," John sighed. "Looks like I'll just have to kill you for it."

"That's not funny," Sophie cried.

"Good," John grinned. "It wasn't a joke. Do as I say and I'll leave. I can snap you in half, you know."

Heavy with disbelief, Sophie sank to the floor. Cold spread throughout her limbs and she stared, open-mouthed.

I won't stand a chance against him.

"I don't..." she stuttered.

"I'll be needing that compass, Miss. Sorry, Mrs. It's best that you hand it over."

"Where's Wade? What did you do to him?"

"Haven't seen him. The compass, I need it. Give me that stove too."

"And if I say no? You'll just kill me?"

"Course I will and no one will ever know I did. Quickly now, hand them over and I'll be off."

He's mad. He's a madman prowling the woods. Where the hell is Wade! What do I do? What will we do without a compass? Do we have two of them? Shit! Think!

Sophie moved slowly and carefully. She dug out the stove and handed it over. She fought the wild urge to scream. She only wanted to be rid of him. If she gave him what he wanted, surely he would leave them alone.

"Compass," John reminded her.

"I can't find it. Wade must have it," she lied. How would they ever find civilization without it?

"Don't even try to lie. I can see it."

The rectangular compass poked out from a side pocket. Sophie closed her eyes, pulled it out, and passed it over.

"Thanks. See you around!"

John laughed and walked away. He stepped over branches and logs as if he knew the area inside and out until he was gone from sight. Sophie let out a shaky breath and sobbed until her whole body shook.

"Wade," she cried. "Where are you?"

What the hell just happened? Do I look around? Stay here? What do I do? Is Wade hurt?

She jumped as she heard the sound of happy whistling. She jerked her head towards the noise and saw Wade walking along with their two bottles, both full of water. She sprang up and ran to him, relief flooded her system.

"I don't understand. Slow down. He made you give him things?"

"I had to, Wade. He said he'd kill me! We have to go, we need to get the police."

"John threatened you?"

"Yes. How many more times do I need to say it!? We have to go!"

"Let me think," he frowned.

"What is there to think about!? John is obviously mad or dangerous. He's probably a criminal hiding out here. He's on the run or something."

"Sophie, you gave him our compass!"

"I had to! Can't you tell directions by the sun and then we can find our way back?"

Wade fell silent. He gazed off into the dense woods.

"Wade, talk to me. Do we have a spare compass?"

"No, we don't! I don't know what to say. He just turned up and threatened you?"

"Yes. He did. Finish packing the tent up, please. We have to go."

Why do I have the feeling that he doesn't believe me? Does he really think I'd make something like this up?

"Okay, if we don't check-in at the end of the hike, people will come looking for us. I've got a map. I know which way to go, roughly."

"Great. Then let's go."

Sophie pulled at Wade's arm. He brushed her off and stood to pack the tent properly.

We're going to be out here for days yet. What if John follows us? He's bigger than Wade. Stronger too, I bet.

She felt sick with worry. Vomit rose up in her mouth, she swallowed it back down painfully. While Wade struggled into his backpack and almost tipped backward, anxiety nibbled away at her stomach.

She took a look around, searching for movement among the trees. Nothing caught her attention.

"This way," Wade announced. "We'll get to the stream and follow it."

"Okay. Quick then."

At least the stream might hide our footprints, just like in movies.

Sophie stayed inches away from Wade and forced herself to walk faster. Her limbs became tighter and cramped. She was already sweating by the time they both heard the soothing sound of running water.

"It's slippy, watch out," he warned.

She clung to boulders to help her on her descent down the steep drop. She yearned to look up and at least try to enjoy the beautiful scenery, but a frantic nervousness plagued her. Every few seconds, she looked back and feared John might be behind them. Sweat poured down her face as the sun beat down heavily on her back.

"Wade, what if he comes back?" She asked. "We're too visible here, too vulnerable."

"He won't and stop being paranoid," Wade replied.

Paranoid? He doesn't understand. He just doesn't get it. He wouldn't like being threatened like I was.

The two walked in silence along the side of the twisting stream for what felt like miles. Sophie felt as if they were going in spiraling circles and not in one direction.

Does he even know where we're going?

She checked her watch and saw only an hour had passed since they'd left the camp.

"Can we stop a moment for a drink? We didn't even have breakfast," she groaned.

Wade tutted and dropped his pack. He kicked at the ground angrily.

"Best you check the map too," Sophie ventured.

"I know where we're going," he snapped. "It wasn't me who lost the compass."

"I told you he threatened…"

Sophie froze as she heard a rustling in the treeline, John stepped out from behind a tree and winked.

Oh my God, now what? I knew he'd follow us. I knew it. We're in deep shit.

John waved as if he were greeting old friends. He took steady strides towards them.

"Fancy seeing you here! I thought you were visiting the caves?" He smiled widely and to Sophie, it looked more like a leer.

He's mocking us, he's playing a game with us.

"You took our compass," Wade growled. "And did you threaten my wife?"

Sophie watched as Wade's face colored red, a sign that he was furious and trying to hold his emotions in. He took a single step forward towards him.

John sat down on the warm grass and crossed his long legs. He yawned widely and chuckled.

"I did. Yes to both questions, and now I want your food."

He's absolutely insane. What do we do? Just how dangerous is he?

"What?" Wade gasped. Sophie flinched and grabbed his arm tightly.

"Your food or I'll kill you. Both of you and believe me, I will do it."

"I'm not giving you anything. And stop following us!" Wade yelled.

Sophie started to shiver. She clutched at her husband's hands.

"I'll kill you," John pointed to Wade. "And I'll take my time killing her."

Wade stared at him and blinked rapidly. No one moved.

"Just give him the food," Sophie whispered. "Please."

John threw his head back and howled. The sudden bizarre sound made Wade jump and Sophie squeal.

"Wade! Give him the food!" She pleaded.

Wade stood and looked from Sophie to John and back again. The fight left his posture as his face paled in defeat. Slowly, he stepped forward and took the water bottles from his pack. He kicked the food-filled backpack towards John.

"Thanks! Now, get walking. Go on. Leave," John laughed.

He pointed downstream. Wade pulled Sophie along as she staggered to keep upright.

"He's a fucking psycho," Wade muttered. "You were right. He's mad."

This is so bad. What do we do? We're miles from anywhere. Miles from anyone. What do we do?

She wiped tears from her face. The day had begun with bright sunlight, how could it turn so bad in such a short space of time?

"Wade, I'm so scared," she said.

"Just keep walking. We'll get away from him. Can you run?"

"I don't know," she cried as tears flowed.

"Cry later. Can you run?"

"Okay, okay. I think so."

Hand in hand, the two raced along the edge of the stream. Wade ran with thick, heavy breaths, while Sophie panted loudly. Black spots burst in her vision as her head pounded.

"Don't quit," Wade cried.

Don't think, just run. Don't think, just run.

A searing pain burst across her ankle as she fell. She rolled into the water as the breath was knocked out of her.

Wade grabbed at her and dragged her back onto the bank.

"I fell," Sophie gasped.

Blood poured from a deep gash on her ankle, the deep red color mixed with the freshwater like spilled ink.

"It's not broken," Wade said. "A jagged rock or something cut you. The first aid kit is in… Shit, it was in my pack."

Sophie took her own pack off and dug out an old t-shirt. She ripped a thick piece off and wrapped it around the wound.

"I'm okay. Let's just keep going. Where will we sleep tonight?"

"We won't. We'll keep going. I'll take your pack."

She climbed back to her feet, dropped her backpack, and tested her weight. The wound hurt, but she wouldn't let it stop her.

We need to get as far away as we can. We'll hide, anything.

Thick spiky bushes lining the water parted, the sound alerted them both.

No, no no! Not again, please!

John appeared and smiled.

"I'm awful hungry," he said. "You wouldn't have any spare food, would you?"

"This is madness!" Wade yelled. "What the fuck is wrong with you?"

"No need to be nasty," John grinned. "I'm just awful hungry."

Sophie sat down with a thud.

She held her head in her hands and sobbed quietly. A feeling of resignation overwhelmed her, despair, and acceptance.

There's no way out of this. He's going to kill us. No one will ever find our bodies.

"Give him the rest of the food," she mumbled. "It's in my pack. Just give it."

Wade plunged his hand into her backpack and brought out the rest of the pasta packets. He threw them, each one landed scattered at John's feet.

"We have nothing left now. Do you understand, we have nothing left for you to take," Wade said.

"Thanks," John smiled and tipped an imaginary hat. "See you around."

Wade yanked Sophie to her feet.

They walked, heads down, numb with shock.

"Another couple of miles and we'll stop for a drink, we've got a bit of water left. Two protein bars are in my pocket too," Wade told Sophie. "And we can manage on water. As soon as we hit civilization, we'll find the police."

She nodded and they walked in silence. Sophie checked the treeline every twenty steps and turned to look behind her. A cold sense of dread filled her. Even though John had taken everything they had, she still expected to see him.

Off in front, the stream opened up into a large body of clear, calm water. Wade stopped to look at their map.

"I wish we had a boat," she sighed.

"I know where we are, we need to go that way," Wade said and pointed off to the horizon. "Three days, only three days Sophie. We'll be fine."

"What if we start a fire? One search and rescue might see?" She asked.

"What if he sees it?" Wade answered.

"There must be something we can do? Can't we keep trying our phones?"

"No signals out here."

"We should have been more prepared," she mumbled.

"How can anyone prepare for this?"

"What about houses? Someone must live around here. We can go for help."

"No one lives out here," Wade sighed. "Too isolated."

"We need to stop him. Overpower him. This is too messed up. There's two of us, and one of him."

"He looks too strong, he won't come back now, and is it really worth the risk? What if one of us gets hurt?"

"We've got to do something!" Sophie cried.

Wade ignored her and patted his thick jacket. With a wide smile, he pulled out a single chocolate bar and held it up like a trophy.

"I forgot I had this!" He laughed.

Sophie's stomach growled loudly. The sound almost made her laugh. For a brief moment, her spirits rose.

We can do this, we can get through this. Imagine the story we'll get to tell our friends!

"Are you not sharing?" John shouted.

Sophie felt her blood turn to ice as fear engulfed her.

Their enemy emerged from the trees and smiled warmly.

"I'm ravenous, awful hungry. Care to share?"

"Stay away from us!" Wade shouted. "What the hell is wrong with you!?"

"Why are you doing this?" Sophie cried.

John only sat down as if he had all the time in the world. He reached into his jacket and took out a cigarette. He lit it casually and blew his match out.

"Why, how, who, what, where. Folks away say those same words," he said.

"Anyway, I'll take everything you have. Your water, clothes, map. All of it. I'm awful hungry don't you know."

"You're insane," Wade hissed. "We'll die out here."

"I've been here for a very long time and I'm just fine. There's food everywhere if you know how to look," John grinned.

"Then you go and eat it!" Sophie yelled.

"Now, where's the fun in that?" John winked.

Sophie began to feel anger rise up inside of her. Fury began to spike. Her heartbeat thudded loudly in her ears. She turned her face away from John.

"We need to overpower him," she whispered quietly.

Wade widened his eyes and then narrowed them. She felt the shift occur in him. His defeated posture straightened, his nod almost imperceptible.

"You can have it all," Sophie shouted. "Just take it and leave us alone."

"Bring it here then," John smirked.

Sophie did as she was asked. She took two steps towards John and stopped.

Do something Wade Please! Now!

Except Wade wasn't moving. Instead, he lowered his head in defeat. She took another step forward and dropped the pack.

"Sorry," she mumbled. "My hands are shaking."

If he won't do anything, I will.

As John tutted and sighed, Sophie's hand landed on a decent-sized rock that had caught her eye.

One chance, you have one chance.

As fast as she could manage, she brought her arm up and aimed. John swung towards her as the rock connected with his forehead. A resounding crack filled the still air.

"NOW!" Sophie screamed. She grabbed the pack and swung it. The impact knocked an already stunned John down onto his back.

Wade appeared and stamped down on his stomach. John shrieked in pain and kicked out. Wade stamped down harder.

Sophie snapped. Her hand felt for another rock, her instinct fuelled her. She grabbed one of several dotted around and jumped up. With all the force she could manage, she brought it crashing down on John's head. She lifted and smashed it down again.

Blood and brain matter splattered over the grass.

Again! Her mind screamed. *Again, again.*

John's features exploded with each impact. Teeth scattered and bounced away. His nose cracked and shattered.

"STOP!" Wade cried. "Sophie stop! He's dead!"

Sophie dropped to her knees, panting and shaking.

I've killed him, I've killed a man. Oh my God! What have I done?

Wade wrapped his arms around his wife as she sobbed and cried. Adrenaline flooded her system, she could not help but feel relieved the man was dead. She peered at the body.

One of his eyes remained left to stare at the clear blue sky.

Serves him right.

She jumped up and ran to the stream, ashamed of herself. She scrubbed at her hands and watched John's blood flow away.

Sophie shuffled along. Her body felt bitterly cold. So cold that she thought she might never be warm again.

"Had to kill him," she mumbled, more to herself. "I had to kill him."

"Sophie, sit down."

Wade held her shoulders and pushed her down slowly so she could rest on a fallen log. They'd walked for an hour to find a clearing and to get away from John's body. Wade carried their remaining pack. He felt worried about his wife and supposed she must be in shock.

"Had to kill him," Sophie repeated.

"The police will understand," Wade reassured her. "We'll tell them everything."

"Had to kill him."

"I know you did. Self-defense. He's probably killed others."

Sophie's body shook, her teeth chattered as Wade placed a mug of hot soup in her hands. She saw that he'd dug a firepit but she couldn't remember watching him do it. Time felt jagged in her mind.

I had to do it. Didn't I? Why is it almost dark? Wasn't it just light?

For her, one moment she saw Wade empty the tent from their own pack John had possession of, the next moment, the tent was ready.

"Come on," he insisted. "Get inside and get warm. Sleep will help. We're safe."

Sophie felt herself being pulled along and into the tent. She thought of getting changed and decided she didn't have the energy. Wade lay beside her and covered her with a sleeping bag.

"You did what I couldn't do, I'm proud of you," he said.

"Had to kill him."

"Yes. Yes, you did."

She felt a tear make its way down her face. It splashed onto her sleeping bag in a single heavy drop.

Did I have to kill him, really? Would he have really hurt us? I'll go to prison, they'll put me in prison.

Wade held her as she cried.

She lay wide awake while her new husband snored softly behind her. She jerked as she heard the sound of breaking wood from the forest surrounding them.

"Wade." She hissed. "I think…"

The closed zip on the tent began to move.

An unbearable few seconds passed as the zip worked its way up slowly.

The flaps were pushed apart. Wade gasped and fumbled for his torch in the darkness.

John peered in.

His face was complete, his skull intact, no wounds, no blood.

An impossible sight.

"Hello. Fancy seeing you again," he smiled. "You haven't got any food, have you? I'm awful hungry."

Sophie screamed, a wail of desperation and confusion. Wade lashed out with a sudden fury. He kicked John and kept kicking until the tent swayed and collapsed. Sophie heard ripping sounds and agonized cries. She curled herself into a ball in terror.

This is impossible! How can he be alive?

"Get away from us!" Wade yelled.

The sound of John laughing echoed from far off.

"He's gone, Sophie. He ran," Wade said as he shook her. "He must have a twin or something? This is…the tents destroyed. This is so fucked up. Come on up. NOW!"

"I can't," Sophie whispered. A light hit her eyes, Wade's torch. The tent hung in torn and slashed pieces around her.

"Come on, please," Wade begged. She felt her body being yanked as if she were a doll. Her mind froze, unable to make sense of killing John and of seeing him again.

"We need to go."

Wade shook her viciously and pulled her to her feet. Sophie cried out and battled his arms away.

"I killed him. I killed him!" She groaned. "This can't be real!"

She staggered as if she was drunk.

Manic laughter erupted from the thick, dark woods.

Sophie gagged and bent forward. She retched and vomited all over her boots.

"I'm awful hungry," a voice in the darkness called.

Wade grabbed Sophie's hand and pulled. They ran.

Both stumbled and fell, both rolled and ripped their skin as they ran in the pitch blackness.

Abruptly, Wade stopped with a grunt and skidded down to the ground. John stood facing them.

"Fancy seeing you here," he said. "I'm awful hungry."

John opened his mouth and revealed sharp, brutal, pointed teeth. A deep wailing sound came from inside him. Sophie saw that he was completely naked.

"Who are you?" Wade breathed.

"What are you?" Sophie whispered.

"Ancient. I'm ancient and I'm awful hungry."

John dropped to a crouch as he howled. His back began to ripple, thick movements warped his flesh as his spine popped and tore. A muscled arm with savage claws reached out and swiped at Wade.

Wade scurried backward until he hit a tree.

Sophie clamped her hands over her ears as she screamed in frozen terror.

John's legs elongated, cracked, and popped.

His face bulged, bone structure pushed forward as his nose and mouth grew into a muzzle. He roared as his body changed. Thick, fur-covered skin appeared as muscles and sinew rearranged. Pointed ears sprouted from his head.

He paused his transformation to growl deeply. Blood and drool fell from his sharp teeth. A long tongue lolled from his mouth as he stood, fur-covered and muscular. He leaped onto Wade and savagely tore his clothing and skin.

"NO," Sophie screamed.

Wade wailed in agony. The beast sunk its teeth into his ripped open stomach.

"Run," Wade coughed as blood sprayed from his mouth.

Sophie ran.

Heart pounding, her legs weak and rubbery, she ran harder than ever.

I shouldn't have left him. I just left him. He'd never leave me. What was that? What the hell was that? Please no, don't let it get me. Please, God.

Sophie heard a howl behind her, she turned to look, convinced the beast was upon her. She ran straight into a thick, low-hanging branch. The impact knocked her off her feet.

She lay dazed on the damp grass.

Is this the end? Is this how I die? Where's Wade? Oh, Wade!

She rolled onto her front and tried to climb to her feet.

The ground vibrated underneath her, heavy thuds of the beast approaching. Sophie closed her eyes. It was too late.

The first bite tore a chunk of flesh from her shoulder and neck. She screamed in white-hot agony and passed out.

* * *

Steve, Richard, and Tim walked steadily. Each felt in sync with the other's movements and pace. The three were experienced hikers and each one viewed the Highlands as nothing more than a walk in the park, a warm-up for an upcoming greater hike.

"Shall we set up camp? It's a good spot here," Steve called. The trio came upon a flat piece of land, the ideal place for a campfire and to pitch their tents.

"I'd kill for a beer," Tim laughed. He dropped his pack and sighed with pleasure. "And we need to double the pace tomorrow, lads."

"We're fine as we are. Hey! Is someone over there? Look."

Steve pointed into the dense woodland. It was almost nightfall, but all three saw the outline of a figure walking towards them. A tall man, with a backpack and a long brown beard. He was alone, but he looked friendly enough.

"Hello!" He called and waved.

"Sorry to bother you. You haven't got any spare food, have you? I'm awful hungry."

Printed in Great Britain
by Amazon